OLD

Jeremy Megargee

OLD HOLLOW FIRST EDITION

ISBN-13: 978-1532748592

ISBN-10: 1532748590

www.facebook.com/JMHorrorFiction

Cover design by MNS Art Studio

For Cerberus, my little guardian of the gates of the Underworld. I will always miss you…

"There is pleasure in the pathless woods, there is rapture in the lonely shore, there is society where none intrudes, by the deep sea, and music in its roar; I love not Man the less, but Nature more."

- Lord Byron

1

Asher

I guess I've always appreciated solitude. It feels like a part of who I am, something that's etched into my DNA. I don't hate people. I don't even really dislike people. People just drain me. I came into this world without social butterfly wings, and I'm okay with that. I think the world needs people like me. The ones who would rather listen instead of talk, the ones who think and imagine...and dare to dream. Old friends used to tell me that I spend too much time in my own head, but if I'm being honest, my own head is one of my favorite travel destinations.

I like the quiet, always have. I guess that's why I enjoy it up here on North Mountain. I get to watch the sun setting behind the pines as twilight fades. I get to listen to the coyotes singing mournful songs in the distant hills. Hearing the crickets chirping, my fire crackling, even the sound of the moths bouncing off the porch light. It's all night music to me. It soothes that part of me that has always longed for wild places. They're rare, places like this. The kind of remote regions that make big cities seem like fables in comparison.

My only neighbors are the trees, towering oaks, sap-smeared pines, and those weeping willows that sway so beautifully when the breeze is just right. It's unusual to want these things, I suppose. It's 2016 and this world is plugged into the conduit of social media, high definition televisions, even hoverboards that celebrities like to show off on in viral videos before inevitably busting their asses. It's the rat race, the age of the consumer. I'm just not made for it. I'm still young, barely thirty now, but my soul feels ancient. It's a soul that clamors for the simple things. A warm fire, a soft bed, and stack of books to keep me company. Who am I to deny the desires of my own soul?

I guess there are words for people like me. Recluse. Introvert. Hermit. Those words don't bother me much. I'm happy here in the forest. I'm happy with the humble little life that I've built for myself. The ridges are my streets. The gulches are my sidewalks. The mountain streams are my swimming pools when the weather gets hot. This wilderness has given me everything that I want out of life.

I come down off the mountain to go into town once in awhile, mostly just for provisions and to visit the local library. Old Hollow isn't even much of a town in the traditional sense. It's in Berkeley County, but it's hard to find on any map of West Virginia, just a little gnat of a place in the valleys beneath North Mountain. The population is under two hundred people, and the only real businesses of note are the post office, the general store, the library and the salvage yard. It's so isolated in the hills that barely any outsiders come through. It's one of those quintessential American backwaters where everyone knows everyone and change or unconformity is looked at like a rattlesnake with venom dripping from its fangs. That's just the way it is with mountain folk. Most of them were born in Old Hollow; most of them will die and be buried in Old Hollow.

It's a forgotten town beneath a lonely mountain. And as far as I'm concerned, it's a good place to put down roots for a man who just wants to be left alone.

***

The mountain streams tend to run slowly, the water babbling and serene, little minnows cruising beneath a perfectly clear reflective surface. Life up here seems to follow the same format. The days are long and sometimes boring, but the serenity makes it all worthwhile. My lifestyle is about as self-sustaining as it can possibly be. The majority of my food comes from hunting and fishing. My warmth comes from a black cast iron woodstove in the center of the cabin. My lullabies come from the wind through the pines and the frogs that chirp in the marshes to the east. I guess this kind of life would be purgatory to some, but it's always been paradise to me.

There's a brook beneath a ridge just a few miles away from the cabin and it's one of the best fishing holes I've ever found up here. It's my special spot and it always seems to be teeming with smallmouth bass. I'm heading up there now with the sun just starting to set on the horizon, my rod and tackle strapped to my back. There's a little waterfall that comes down from the ridge and feeds into the brook, creating a shallow pond that always seems to catch the fading sunlight and turn it into a blaze of shimmering orange.

There's beauty here, but there are also memories. I recall one morning ages ago—almost nine years if I'm doing the math correctly—I stumbled across a sight that tore the breath right out of my throat. It was just after dawn broke, a misty day with almost no visibility in sight. I woke up extra early and already had a great haul at my special spot, several smallmouth bass and even one fat catfish strung up across my shoulder. I was turning around to head for home when I spotted her there, a few ferns brushing up against her flanks.

I noticed the eyes first. Those deep, golden eyes watching me cautiously as she lapped at the water in the brook. I'd seen pictures of mountain lions before, but seeing one in the flesh is a different experience entirely. There was something majestic about the poise of her, the way she held her shoulders while she drank. I guess the biggest shock of all was the fact that she was up here on North Mountain at all. There've been sporadic cougar sightings in West Virginia over the years, but most of them are considered tall tales since the big cat is said to be extirpated in this part of the country.

But there she was, defying all the odds. I felt an entire mixture of emotions as I watched her and she watched me. There was fear, awe, and an undercurrent of pity that dominated the other feelings. I could tell just by looking at her that she was in a poor state. She was young, barely older than a cub...and she looked close to starvation. Her body was practically skeletal, the ribs standing out harshly against her coat. She showed no fear of me, only a mild curiosity.

I couldn't tell you how long we stood there watching each other. Maybe it was only seconds, but it was one of those rare times in life where it felt like eternity was rolling on by. She finished drinking the water, licking her chops afterwards. Her nose sniffed the air, seeming to detect that fishy scent emanating from my morning catch. What I did next just came naturally. I unhooked half of the smallmouth bass and even the prize catfish, and I threw it across the water towards her. They landed barely a foot away with a dull splat, and automatically she was on them, greedily snapping up the meal. I'd guess it was the first meal she'd had in a long, long time.

She licked every scrap of skin and fish bone from her black lips, and then she set those golden eyes upon me once again. Something seemed to pass between me and that animal. I can't find the right words for it, but it felt powerful. It was like this unspoken connection between man and beast, a brief window where I felt like the wilderness itself had delved into the fibers of my heart.

It didn't last. Moments like that never last. She finally just loped off into the underbrush and after awhile I started back home. I never saw her again, but every time I come to this spot I can't help but think about what became of her. The pessimist in me thinks that she died somewhere out there in the forest, but the optimist says that maybe she carved out a piece of territory deeper in the rocky regions and maybe she's still out there to this day, hunting and surviving.

That's a large part of life out here for all of us, animal and man alike. We hunt and we survive. We take what the land has to offer us and we make due. That's the duality of nature, the ability to be fantastically cruel and fantastically benevolent all at the same time.

I cast my line while I'm letting these old memories swirl in my head. It doesn't take long before I get a bite.

2

Asher

I'm lying in bed with my belly still warm from the meal of fish and potatoes I just finished. I feel languid and wholly at peace, my calf muscles still burning a bit from today's hike up the mountain trails. The Charles Bukowski collection I'm reading takes my mind off the stinging sensation in my muscles. For a time I'm lost in his tales of boozing and whoring and raising the most wonderful kind of hell. Bukowski lived in a humble haze with almost no possessions to his name in his youth, but he still left a scorched mark on the world when he passed. He wrote whatever poured out of the depths of his soul—sometimes sour, sometimes sad, but always infinitely interesting. I like writers like him best of all. The ones that give you everything with just a few words on a page, every single fiber of themselves, the good and the bad. Honesty laid bare, the vulnerability of being a human animal on this crazy spinning mudball we call planet Earth.

I use a dried oak leaf as a bookmark before shelving the title. I'm a bigger guy, mostly on the tall side—and splitting wood for decades has given me arm definition that most gym rats can only dream of—so it's always a precarious climb when I make my way up the ladder to my loft. I make it there without smashing my skull into the cabin ceiling, so I consider that a win. I turned the light off before heading up, but my cot is still bathed in an orange glow as I lie down and get comfortable. It's a gleaming amber light that filters in through the loft's little circular window.

It's the brightest, fullest harvest moon I've seen in a long time. It seems to dominate the sky, making the stars seem like insignificant pinpricks in comparison. It's so damn close I can see just about every crater on the surface, and if I were so inclined I feel like I could open the window and touch that pitted moon-face. It hits me hard that summer has ended, autumn becoming a reality now. This great, looming moon seems almost to grin in response to my thought, foretelling that very cold, long nights wait in the near future.

I close my eyes and focus on resting. At some point after midnight a thunderstorm touches down, lightning streaking through the heavens and powerful booms ripping through the mountain valleys. For one drowsy moment it almost sounds like gunfire and screaming below the mountain, perhaps somewhere way down there in the streets of Old Hollow. The mind has a funny way of bringing sounds to your ears when you're just a breath or two away from deep REM sleep.

At an undetermined time during the ravaging melodies of the storm, slumber finally takes me. It pulls me in like a lover with soft, silky lips, and I can't help but succumb.

***

I awaken late the next day sometime just before noon. I'll be going into town today, mostly to replenish my canned food stock and return a few library books. It's a rare occurrence for me, one I try to limit as much as possible. The townsfolk know of me, I wouldn't necessarily say they're wary of me, but they see me as an oddball. I guess the concept of living in solitude just doesn't compute for most people. They might not drive me away with pitchforks and torches, but their shrewd eyes often send unspoken words in my direction as I walk the streets while running errands. I sometimes imagine what they might be thinking just to amuse myself.

"There goes that whacky hermit."

"I'd better steer clear of that black-bearded mountain inbred!"

"What a godless pagan living up there all alone in those hills..."

Sometimes it's hard to suppress a chuckle when the old-timers glare at me with those hard, stubborn gazes. It can't be helped. People in small towns like Old Hollow have nothing to do with their time but talk, and being suspicious of a man who likes his privacy is just another topic to gab about as they stand around the kerosene stove in the back of the general store. It's the small-town equivalent of water cooler gossip, except the office space tends to be plowed fields and sagging porches as opposed to some building full of cushy cubicles.

I pile my books into a leather satchel across my back and climb onto the seat of my trusty ATV. It's a battered old beast, the paint peeling and the tires a little worn, but it's the best transportation I could ever ask for up here. It tears across the rough terrain with a determination I can't help but admire, and I'd likely consider it one of the most essential machines I have with me at the cabin.

The ATV fires up with a smooth purring sound, and I start down the dirt path that cuts into the road down the mountain a few miles in the distance. There's only one paved road leading down from North Mountain, the asphalt extremely narrow and in pitiful disrepair. It's only used occasionally by hunters and hikers, so the state doesn't make it a priority on the road maintenance list. It's a bumpy ride down the dirt trails before I finally hit the fissured asphalt, and then the ride gets even bumpier.

My ears pop as the elevation changes, the road curving downward in a steep, snaking twist. I can see most of Old Hollow above the treetops, the town stretched out down there in the valley like a miniature oil painting. I see a few gusts of smoke drifting up here and there across the entire length of the town. It's not uncommon for people to burn brush and garbage in barrels and pits on their property in town; it's actually something that most people do on a frequent basis when junk starts piling up.

It seems strange, though. It's a windy day, not the best weather conditions for brush fires. My eyes lock on those pluming tendrils of smoke curling up into the atmosphere beyond the mountain's summit. A nagging question starts to eat at me.

Why so many fires?

3

Asher

It doesn't take long for the narrow lane down North Mountain to become Route 56, the main road that cuts through town. I'm taking it slow now, the ATV barely crawling along. I feel a little sweat dripping down the back of my neck even though the day isn't particularly hot. Something feels fundamentally wrong. I can't explain it other than just pure instinct infecting every fiber of my body. I know the sounds of Old Hollow. I've been driving into this little nowhere town for decades now, the map and flow of the town something that is all too familiar to me. You'll hear old men chattering on porches. You'll hear wreckers lugging dead automobiles around at the salvage yard. You'll hear bluegrass music drifting out of open windows and lawnmowers tearing up fresh, lush grass.

I hear none of those sounds now. None of the sounds that are just as big a part of Old Hollow as the very ground it's built upon. There's a silence here now, a silence that feels oppressive and foreign to me. A few sounds manage to permeate that thick blanket of quiet, but they inspire no confidence. I hear the sizzling of flames. I hear little tearing noises like vultures pecking at carrion.

Sound becomes less important as I round the bend and finally get free of the trees, my sightline becoming clear. That's when I bring the ATV to a totally unexpected stop. Hearing what might lie ahead was bad, but seeing what lies ahead...is so much worse. It's enough to make my eyes feel dry in the sockets. It's like driving straight into Hell without even realizing that you were approaching the gates.

Old Hollow lies in smoking ruin. It has the look of a place that has been gutted, absolutely violated. Some of the houses along Main Street are blazing still, the flames just now starting to die down. It becomes clear that some of them have been allowed to burn all night. The buildings that haven't been touched by infernos aren't in much better condition. Windows are shattered, strong wooden doors look busted inward, these homes and businesses looking much like ravaged remnants of the safe havens they once were.

This couldn't have been caused by the storm last night, could it? I can't believe that. The storm was mild as far as thunderstorms go in these parts. Something else has happened here. This is pure, systematic destruction.

I dismount from the ATV and decide to explore on foot a bit, the enigma of Old Hollow's fall already starting to chew on my soul. Could it have been some other natural disaster? Earthquake? Twister? No. I don't think that's right.

I'm walking past the post office now, the front of the building plastered in bullet holes. A large mail truck outside looks like it was shredded with a chainsaw, the side of the truck sporting a torn crater with letters tumbling outward and being carried across the streets by the breeze.

The smoke obscures my visibility a little, but in a few more yards I come to a Sedan rolled over in the middle of the street. The windshield is obliterated and the driver's side door seems to have been ripped completely off. I finally notice it lying discarded in the grass a few yards away.

There's a body lying next to the overturned car. I approach him cautiously, my heart beating wildly in my chest. I'm looking down at the face of a corpse that I immediately recognize. I never knew the man personally, but I know he owned a horse farm a little further along Route 56. I wish I could recall his name. Somehow the car's battery hasn't died yet and the radio is still playing as I crouch down next to the corpse. It's an old Johnny Cash tune, "The Beast in Me."

It's hard to look at this man. It's hard to look at what's left of this man. His knee is nothing but splattered meat, looking almost like it took a high caliber round at close range. It's his torso that stays with me, lurking in my head and making my stomach turn. He's been completely disemboweled; his intestines sprawled out across the road in little pink spirals.

I struggle to keep my breakfast in my stomach, and I try to do the man a service by reaching out to close his eyelids. My fingertips stop centimeters away from his irises. The eyes have lazily rolled over to look at me. Somehow, this tattered soul...is still alive.

His lips are moving, parched and bleeding, but trying hard to form whispered words. I lean down to him as close as I dare, my ear canal taking in the sound of his wheezy, final breaths.

"They came...in the night," he rasps, plasma oozing out of the corner of his mouth to stain his stubbly chin.

"Who came? Who did this to you?" The question sounds dry and uncertain coming out of my mouth.

The man's eyes blink desperately. He seems beyond delirious. Almost beyond everything.

"They killed the town. They kill everything."

The man lets this statement hang in the smoky air. His next intake of breath sounds strained, full of gurgling wetness.

"The pale one...is the worst. It happened so fast. I was just driving to—"

Coughing puts this comment to rest, a fine speckling of blood splattering up against my face.

"Just stay still. I'm gonna get you help..." The statement feels impotent the moment I say it. This man is far past the point of help.

"Please...don't let them get to my boy. He's...seven now. He loves to draw...he always draws...the horses..."

I'm forced to watch as the last of the light leaves this man's eyes. He breathes once or twice more, snuffling breaths, and then it's over. Mercifully, I reach out with a trembling hand to close those determined eyes.

I kneel at his side for a long time. I've never seen the death of another human being this close up before. It's a strange feeling. It rattles something inside of me, leaves me feeling hollow and raw.

The specter of Death hangs heavy over Old Hollow at this particular moment in time. I have a sick feeling in the pit of my stomach that he'll be staying awhile...

4

The Night Before

Edna's eyes flicker open, the blankets twisted up around her aching legs. She was dreaming about Martin. Not that husk in the hospital bed all eaten up with cancer—as he'd been in his final days—but that young, handsome soldier that had swept her off her feet such a long time ago. She regrets waking up from a dream that sweet. She doesn't sleep enough as it is at her age, so every precious hour counts.

At first she thinks the storm woke her, but it seems the rain has died down outside. She barely hears a drizzle on the rooftop now. She's hearing lots of strange noises coming from the outside of the house. It almost sounds like people yelling at each other. She picks her hearing aide up and places it into her right ear, turning the volume to the maximum, but still she can't make out exactly what all the commotion is. Mayhap just some domestic dispute in this ungodly hour of the night. Her neighbors—that damned Banner couple—seem to get into it at all hours sometimes, especially when an eighty four year old woman is trying to get to sleep at a normal hour. That's young love for you, so much passion in those two spitfires they could star in their own soap opera.

Edna sits up in bed, already reaching for her bifocals on the nightstand. She just got them last week and she's still adjusting to the extra thick lenses. Every part of her hurts, just dull aches and pains, the result of spending too many decades in one tired old body. She's got a mind to take a hickory switch to Roy Banner's ass if that is him hollering and raising hell outside of her home.

She slips her feet into her slippers, taking a moment to examine the wrinkles and varicose veins on her own skin. Time just doesn't have a scrap of empathy for a senior citizen. It just rolls right on, a remorseless wheel.

She fetches her cane last of all, using it to totter out of her bedroom towards the bay windows in the living room. She sweeps the curtain aside with a hand that twitches with arthritis.

Her eyes widen behind the bifocals, the faded brown irises reflecting distant firelight.

She must still be dreaming. That's the only explanation for what she sees out there. Across the street she can just make out a dark figure strolling along with a red can and a lit torch. The figure casually splashes the liquid from the can all over the front of the Banner cottage...and then he tips the torch down right on the exterior wall. The cottage blooms into an orange firestorm. The figure moves on down the street, and if Edna's ears don't deceive her, he seems to be *whistling.*

She finds the courage to pull the door open just as something catches her attention down near the post office. It's a high, desperate screaming that makes her want to turn down the volume on her hearing aide. It sounds like Marla Bishop, that teacher who moved here from Inwood. Edna squints her eyes past the elm tree in her yard, and sure enough Marla is running wildly down the road, her bare feet slapping the asphalt. Some man runs behind her, loping like a deer, a tool of a sort held in his hand. It's too far away for Edna to be sure, but it looks like the man is holding a hatchet. What in the name of the Heavenly Father is happening out there?

Edna's attention is suddenly diverted by the sound of the old tire swing creaking in her front yard. It's been there ages, supported by the strongest limb of the elm on her property. Sometimes her grandchildren like to play on it.

There's some woman swinging on it now. She wears all black so she's hard to see, but her hair looks kinda chopped up, long on one side and shaved on the other, one of those trendy styles. Edna struggles to make out the woman's features, but she can't discern much. Inky shadows seem almost to cling to her as she swings back and forth, kicking her legs for momentum.

Edna finds her voice, her words coming out a little slurred without her dentures in.

"Who are you?"

The question is met with a giggle. There's something in that giggle that Edna doesn't like. When Edna was a little girl her mom used to take her to visit an estranged aunt at some asylum in Virginia. She remembers most of the people in that loony bin used to giggle in the exact same way that this woman does.

The laughter dies away, and the woman's voice comes out in a singsong tone. It sounds jovial, carefree. It's a voice that is tinged with excitement.

"Just a visitor." She says, her legs kicking out again as she swings even higher.

Edna is starting to feel a slow burning dread in the center of her frail chest. She reaches up to touch the crucifix around her neck, but then she remembers that she left it on the nightstand next to her bed.

"Well...what do you want?"

Edna has barely asked this question when things start to happen very fast. There's a crash from behind her, something impossibly large and strong smashing into the back door. She hears lamps falling to the rug and footsteps so forceful that they seem to crack the tile of her kitchen floor. She tries to turn around, but the woman on the swing distracts her, finally answering her question.

"Oblivion." It's said with that same hint of glee, and Edna sees a flash of the woman's turquoise eyes as she swings so high that the moonlight briefly touches her face.

Something slams into Edna from behind, her cane falling from her hand. There's a choked, brittle scream and the sound of flesh being torn, shredded, absolutely eviscerated. Wet sounds follow. Gurgling sounds like chewing and splattering, a body being transformed into nothing but ribbons of pliable meat.

Edna's bifocals fall down to hit her Welcome Home mat before bouncing off and flying across the yard. They come to rest in the grass near the tire swing. The woman reaches down and picks them up, noticing the one cracked lens and the blood that's smeared all over them.

The woman finally stops swinging...and she places the blood-soaked bifocals over her own eyes. She giggles again, looking out at the mayhem unfolding in the streets of Old Hollow.

"It's so beautiful, Endre. The world looks all red..."

The wet, ragged sounds continue behind her. The woman spends a long time just enjoying the view.

***

Havoc follows. The nightfall enshrouds it, distant screams echoing across the valley. There is whispered pleading in pitch black rooms and transformers exploding with sparks after being shot or torn from utility poles. The town's one and only cell tower is now a burning stake beyond Mill Street. An electrician is chained to the tower, almost crucified there. He burns right along with the tower, the melting metal finally dripping down to slither across his blackened skull.

A naked man stumbles across the general store's parking lot, his eyes full of horror as he cradles the stump where his left hand used to be. A dark shape flits out from behind a van and hits the man like a missile, driving him out of sight behind the vehicle. There's a sound like something piercing his throat, a sharp appendage being forced directly through his adam's apple, and then we hear no more.

Two hunters have roused themselves enough to try and combat whatever force is destroying their town, both grizzled men standing back to back with rifles in hand near the front of the historical society. Something makes a sound near a trashcan in a little alley close to them. Both men fire at once, the impact of their combined gunfire tearing the trashcan to bits and dropping it to one side. A rat scurries out and flees for dear life.

Behind the men, some rising shape lifts the entire weight of a dumpster above its head. The dumpster is thrown so violently that it not only knocks the men down, but it lands directly on top of them, flattening their bodies. One dies with his neck twisted grotesquely to the side. The other dies with the barrel of his own rifle impaled in his abdomen.

There are little acts of rebellion like this occurring all over town, men and women fighting back with everything they have. It doesn't last. They never saw this coming. They never even had a chance.

A child's tricycle lies abandoned in the middle of Main Street, the tassels on the handlebars fluttering in the wind.

From dusk to dawn, Old Hollow goes from quiet sanctuary to dripping abattoir.

The only witness to every little atrocity that occurs tonight is that fat, orange harvest moon sitting high in the sky.

In terms of massacres, the moon seems entirely indifferent.

5

Asher

I manage to pull an emergency road blanket from the Sedan and cover up the man's corpse with it. I'm not sure what else to do until I'm able to find someone with a cell phone to call the proper authorities. That's one of the disadvantages of living off the grid in the mountains, no real reason to own a cell phone because there's no signal that far up in elevation anyways. I can't understand why an ambulance hasn't blazed out here already. This entire section of Main Street should be crawling with police and firefighters by now. So where are they?

And the even more disturbing question to consider, where is *anyone?* The streets are barren in this cradle of carnage, the mutilated man the only human being I've seen thus far since getting into town. The strangest thing is that I don't feel a sense of complete desertion in the town, but instead it's a feeling of wary silence, almost like I'm being watched from hidden alcoves.

I need to get over to the Old Hollow Police Department. It's a squat little brick building near the center of town and only about five officers are employed there, but at least it's something. There has to be an explanation here. An entire town doesn't just fall victim to some sort of catastrophe without some response from law enforcement and medical personnel.

Old Hollow isn't a large town, so I decide to leave my ATV parked for the time being. I can walk to the police station from here. I start my trek down the road, my footsteps sending echoes through the eerily quiet town. There are things I see along the way that unsettle me even more, my head starting to feel like a nest of confusion and budding fear.

A few dangling chains hang from one of the low streetlamps along the sidewalk, a few bits of bones and flesh dangling from the hooked portions of the chains. It almost looks like someone dressed several deer right there in the middle of the street. There's even a lump of discarded guts thrown against a storm drain. I give this area a wide berth, the breeze causing the hooked chains to gently sway back and forth.

Most of the townsfolk in this area prefer big lifted trucks, especially Fords with wheels so big they must be extensions of the driver's egos. I come across one of these trucks smashed headlong into a utility pole. All the wheels are flat and strangest of all; portions of the truck's metal siding seem to have literally been peeled off. There's a ragged hole in the truck's roof, almost man-sized. The metal is torn backwards and shards of it are splashed in some drying liquid the color of rust. Plasma that has faded in the sunlight...

I'm approaching the police station now. I see two squad cars out front, so that's a good sign. It's the first legitimate sign of hope I've felt since I stumbled into this nightmare of a situation. The shades are drawn on the windows so I can't see the interior of the station. I try the door. It's unlocked.

The door opens into darkness.

6

Asher

It takes my eyes a moment to adjust to the lack of illumination in the little station's central lobby. As soon as the darkness dissipates, I wish it back. I will it to return and shield my eyes from the horror that is plastered across the walls. Old Hollow is a tiny town and the police station reflects this, the building relatively small with a single drunk tank cell set far back at the end of a corridor.

I didn't know Sergeant Wilks. I'd seen him once driving down the road in his squad car, but I didn't even know his name then. I only know it now because I'm looking at his name tag. I remember his sandy-colored facial hair and his propensity to wear mirrored aviator sunglasses. I once stood behind him in the general store and he kept the shades on the whole time, never bothering to take them off. I suppose they were a comfort to him.

He wears what remains of those mirrored sunglasses even in death. I see my own reflection glaring back at me from one lens, but where the other lens should be there is only a crater of red gore, a pit full of coagulated blood and tiny white skull fragments. At first I think it a suicide, but there's no sign that the man turned his revolver on himself. It repulses me to even consider the idea, but the missing portion of the Sergeant's head almost looks...*chewed* upon.

His upper torso is mangled in a similar fashion, his uniform shirt shredded and stained in his own life's blood. It's that reddened index fingertip that keeps drawing my attention, though. It seems the man survived his mauling just long enough to scrawl out a messy message on the wall behind him.

It's nothing but a streaked remnant, a warning for those that might be unlucky enough to find him. In this case, it seems I've drawn the short straw.

The words chill my bones. It's a single sentence, one that leads to more questions and no answers.

"Bullets don't stop them..."

There are no signs of the other officers here. If I had to guess most of them responded to the initial wave of whatever the fuck happened in town last night. This place is sanctified by silence, no authority left here, no help. Now it's just a tomb.

Some rattling sound comes from the far back of this tomb I've discovered, the place where that solitary cell is. The sound comes with implications, thoughts and imaginings that turn my blood to ice water in my veins. I delicately remove the late Sergeant's revolver from the holster on his hip, checking very quietly to ensure that there's ammunition in the firearm. There is, every single bullet accounted for. If hunting in the mountains has taught me anything, it's to be very comfortable and proficient with a gun in hand. Also cautious. Extremely cautious.

I start walking along the narrow hallway that leads back to the cell. I'm very aware of my own footfalls, making sure to keep them as quiet as humanly possible. My mind swims with all the dark content I've seen in the media lately, ideas of terrorists and murderers and all that looming fear propaganda. Is something like that happening here? Is *someone* like that waiting for me in the cell back there?

A droplet of sweat rolls into my eyes, but I don't make any move to wipe it away. I keep both hands on the firearm, pointing it forward, the only light a glimmering crimson EXIT sign deeper down the hall. It shows me that something has been pulled across the cell bars, some material like a blanket...hung up there and blocking all sight.

What is this material concealing? What rattles in this station turned tomb?

I can't wait any longer. I swallow down a lump of unease and I tear the blanket away, two figures immediately darting backwards in the cell, clinging to each other. They look at me with wet, terrified eyes. Hair is plastered across both of their foreheads, seemingly soaked in panicked perspiration.

It's a young mother...and her even younger daughter.

7

Asher

It takes me nearly ten minutes to convince the woman that I'm not going to hurt her or her child. She's obviously traumatized, her eyes a flashing green, red-rimmed from tears and lack of sleep. I can barely see the little girl, her face buried against her mom's blouse. I've never seen the woman around town before. She looks to be maybe early thirties with thick blonde hair that cascades past her shoulders. It's silky and golden-hued, framing a pretty bare face that lacks any kind of makeup. A natural beauty even in her panicked state.

She seems to finally gain some vague recognition when it comes to my appearance. Some of the tension leaves the cell as I place the revolver out of sight and sit down on the threadbare cot. The little girl sniffles deeply, reaching up with one tiny hand to wipe her nose.

I finally manage to coax names out of them. The mother is Mallory. The daughter is Cara. I trade my name for theirs.

"You live up on the mountain, don't you?" asks Mallory, her voice low on the sound spectrum, deeply soothing. "I saw you once on an ATV..."

"That's me. Just your friendly neighborhood hermit."

This comment awards me the ghost of a smile from Mallory. It's enough for now. It's promising. Cara still keeps her face hidden, occasionally peeking out to get an eyeful of me.

"What happened to this town, Mallory?"

She just shakes her head, that golden hair flowing from side to side.

"We were asleep. We live out on East Road, not far from the town center. I woke to screams and gunfire. There was this hot, orange light at my window. I didn't realize until I woke Cara and got her outside that the light was my neighbor's trailer burning to the ground..."

She pauses, seeming to relive this moment. I can almost see the memory of firelight glowing in her eyes.

"So people did all this? Who in the hell are they?" Even as the question leaves my lips, I can't wrap my head around the implications.

"I've heard them, but I haven't seen them. Loud, distant voices. It seemed...coordinated. Almost like they'd been planning it for a long time."

Mallory reaches down and brushes a lock of sweaty blonde hair out of her daughter's face.

"Only Cara saw them. We were running blind, fires everywhere, people shouting and confused. Sergeant Wilks waved us into the police station. He took us back to this cell and managed to hang up the blanket. He hid us..."

Mallory chokes back a sob, gleaming tears threatening to spill down her cheeks.

"Cara was peeking out of a hole in the blanket when they came into the station. She saw them. She saw what they did...to Sergeant Wilks..."

The little girl seems to still be in shock, her body trembling just at the thought of what she witnessed. I don't ask her what she saw, but she starts to tell me anyways, her voice coming out in choppy whispers, almost like if she doesn't get the words out of her then she'll just wither inside.

"One was old and dirty. The other one was tall and had dark skin, no hair on his head." Cara explains, her fingers gripping tightly to Mallory's blouse.

"Did they say anything, Cara?" I can't help but ask. Maybe it'll help us somehow if we know more about all of this.

"The old one said some bad words. The tall one didn't say anything."

A lump forms in Cara's throat as she swallows deeply.

"The policeman had a big gun. He had a big shotgun. I heard the boom when he shot the old one in the chest..."

Mallory caresses the top of her daughter's head.

"You don't have to tell us, honey." Cara shakes her off though, plunging ahead, trying to purge the memories out of her head.

"I thought the old man would die. People always die in the movies when they get shot like that. He stumbled...but that was all. Then he laughed. His laugh is scary."

Cara becomes deathly still for a moment, her fingers drifting to the cold floor of the cell, digging at one of the grooves there.

"What did they do then, Cara?" I already know, but for some odd reason I think maybe hearing it said out loud will make some sort of sense.

"They...they...ate him up. They ate the policeman up."

Cara finally breaks down, tears oozing down her cheeks. She buries her face in her own small hands now, Mallory doing what she can to soothe her daughter. I reach out tentatively to place a hand on Mallory's shoulder, lowering my voice as best I can.

"Do you have a cell phone?"

Mallory nods, but there's no hope in her facial expression.

"No signal. A few hours ago I got the Sergeant's phone out of his pocket...same thing. The landline is dead too."

I scrub a hand across my forehead, momentarily at a loss. Mallory's voice brings me out of my haze and back to grim reality.

"What do you think these people want, Asher? Why are they doing this?"

My mind races. Maniacs. Cannibals. People gone utterly mad. I can't even begin to put this puzzle together. I give Mallory the only answer I have, an honest one, but one that offers no great insight or comfort.

"I wish I knew..."

8

Salvage Yard (Den)

The boy stands next to the hill comprised of nude corpses. It can't really be described as just a pile now because it's so towering and elevated, a literal mound of dead bodies in the center of the salvage yard. He watches The Twins build up a bonfire a few feet away, adding large scraps of lumber from all over the area. The Twins carry out this action in total silence, just as they do with everything else. The boy isn't sure if they were born without vocal cords or suffered some accident later in their lives, but they've been completely mute for as long as he's traveled with them. They communicate with a moleskin pad and pen shared between them, just as they share everything in life.

The boy is momentarily captivated by the ritualistic scars on the foreheads of The Twins. His eyes crawl over the patterns, the deep grooves embedded in the dark skin of their hairless heads. He once asked Jok about them out of pure curiosity. He can only tell Jok apart from Thon by the red birthmark on the side of his bicep, otherwise they're totally identical. Jok spent quite awhile scrawling out his answer on the pad. He showed the boy his response, explaining that it's a common tribal practice in the Sudan, particularly with the Dinka tribe that Jok and Thon come from. He said the tribe's "sorcerer" took a heated blade to their heads and carved the patterns in, helping them to transition from boyhood to manhood.

It's an unsettling thought. The boy has experienced many unsettling thoughts since he began traveling with this group and learning their practices. He turns his gaze to Raymond now, watching the filthy old-timer rolling another body towards the hill of corpses, this one just the upper half of a female torso. The woman was particularly corpulent, so the old bastard struggles, a grimace formed across what can be seen of his mouth within that tangled salt and pepper beard.

"JOK! How about you help me roll what's left of this fat bitch to the pile?"

Jok leaves his brother to tend the fire, heading over to assist the old man.

The old man's beady eyes fall on the boy as well, that gaze seething and untrustworthy. In the short time that he's been with this group, the boy has come to loathe Raymond most of all.

"You too, little shit. Come earn your keep and quit all that loafing around on your skinny ass all day."

The boy reluctantly rises to his feet, moving over to help Raymond and Jok roll the mutilated torso to the bottom portion of the corpse-hill.

"Why are we piling them up like this here?" The boy can't help but ask, all of this so foreign to him.

"We're staying here awhile longer, and Endre has decided this place is as good as any to make camp. We gotta have rations. I'll be damned if we're fixing to starve in this little shit-splat of a town..." Raymond replies, acting like the boy just asked the most stupid, obvious question ever.

The boy crouches next to the pile, wiping blood from the torso off on his tattered jeans.

"Where is Endre?"

Raymond points one dirty finger up towards the brick building in the distance beyond a few stacks of crushed automobiles. It served as the salvage yard's garage and office before the sacking of the town.

"He's up there fuckin' Lizzie's brains out right now, if you want my guess. Endre gets mighty horny after the first night of a Feast. Just thank your lucky stars he's got that crazy loon to stick his meatstick into...otherwise he might give you a go, kiddo."

Raymond smiles that smeared smile of his, most of his teeth brown and rotten, his breath reeking of gore and stale tobacco. Jok simply shakes his head, moving back to assist his brother with the bonfire. The Twins seem to ignore Raymond's disgusting musings most of the time, but since the boy is the lowest man on the totem pole now, Raymond seems to enjoy playing with him and instilling dread in his young heart.

"I saw you peeking at Lizzie the other day when she was leaning over to pick something up. Seems you got an eyeful of that ass crack showing in her tight leather pants. You got a little crush on Endre's favorite slut, Grady?"

The boy's cheeks heat up as he blushes. He turns his eyes to the ground.

"I wasn't doing that. You don't know what you're talking about."

Raymond laughs. His laugh is just as repulsive as him, choked with tar and bits of meat gristle.

"Don't even fuckin' lie. I saw you. Let's just hope Endre never sees it...because if he does, he'll open you up from groin to gullet."

Raymond keeps laughing, and as he walks by he slaps Grady hard on the back of the skull, hard enough to bring a misty sheen to the boy's eyes. Grady doesn't give him the satisfaction of actually crying. Abuse like this has been frequent since he joined them. He's almost used to it by now.

Grady turns his attention away from Raymond, the old man stumbling off to take a piss somewhere. He turns his eyes to Thon crouched there by the burning timber. Thon is heartlessly cold when it comes to the victims, but he seems thoughtful around Grady.

"What happens next, Thon?"

Thon stands, rising up to his full height, all gangly limbs and massive scarred forehead. He takes some time to scrawl in his notepad, his dark eyes flashing with intelligence. He finally tears off a page and hands it to Grady.

"We set up bait traps. There are many still in hiding. We need to draw them out and finish them. We leave only when the town is gutted. Sniff the air...you'll smell the ones still out there, hiding and sweating."

The boy reads the message, and then he drops the piece of paper, the breeze carrying it down to the bonfire where it turns ashen, the corners blackening.

Grady sniffs the air, his nostrils expanding.

Thon is right.

He does smell them...

***

Night has fallen, the sky a pitch black canvas of bright pinprick stars. The bonfire rages now, almost everyone standing around it in a circle. The Twins stare into the flames quietly, seeming almost contemplative. Raymond noisily swirls chewing tobacco between his lips. Grady sits a little further back on an overturned refrigerator, the boy nervously fidgeting with his hands. They're waiting for Endre. They're waiting for the next phase.

There's finally noise from the garage, but the footfalls are light and graceful. Lizzie skips onto the scene, clad in tight leather pants and a white tank top tied across her flat tummy, a tattoo of a serpent encircling her navel and swallowing its tail seeming to feature extra glossy in the firelight. Lizzie has the features of a pretty pixie, her face heart-shaped and dominated by flashing turquoise eyes. At first glance she seems just like a harmless punker, but if you take time to see exactly what flashes in those eyes; you realize she's anything but harmless. Lunacy lives in little Lizzie, and it manifests itself in a variety of different ways, making her one of the most unpredictable members of the group...and Endre's favorite pet.

She gazes up at the corpse-hill, her mouth falling agape, those ruby-stained lips looking plump and raw from Endre's rough kisses.

"Wow, boys...you've made a mountain! It's the biggest, tallest mountain around. It's our mountain. We should climb it!"

Lizzie blossoms with enthusiasm, just like usual. She grabs hold of Raymond's hand and tugs him towards the corpse-hill, but he lightly shrugs her off, turning back to the piece of nameless meat that turns on a steel skewer above the fire.

"No fun. Tired old Raymond...never even an ounce of fun." She giggles as she says this, already heading for the corpse-hill, climbing and clawing against the dead bodies, her movements graceful and cat-like. She finally reaches the summit, a few severed limbs tumbling down the hill as she sits down on top and gets comfortable. Grady can't help but watch her, something almost alluring about the woman's madness.

Raymond finally pulls the piece of charred meat from the fire, proceeding to sink his ruined teeth into it. He pulls a hot chunk down his throat, relishing the taste. His bubbly old voice finds its way up to Lizzie on the corpse-hill.

"Where's Endre? Our cattle are starting to get a little restless back there in their jailhouse."

Raymond gestures to an ancient van near the center of the camp. It has no tires at all, sitting directly on the ground. The side door is open but it's strung up with barbwire netting and all the windows and escape points are nailed closed with sheet metal. Two sweaty, terrified faces stare out from the barbwire, their fingers entwined around the barrier that keeps them in this makeshift cage. They appear to be a couple, a young husband and an equally young wife. They cling desperately to each other, keeping as silent as possible. They learned the hard way that screaming isn't tolerated among the people that hold them captive here.

Before Lizzie has time to answer, there's a loud clamor as one of the garage doors slams open. A large, towering man starts to stalk his way towards the bonfire. The skeleton of an old Ford Pinto is in his way, so the man casually reaches down and flips it over his shoulder...the entire weight of the car crashing down behind him. Grady watches this in awe, the car seeming like just a small feather to Endre. The boy has come to experience awe almost each time he interacts with Endre. Awe...and a bone-deep fear that makes his stomach churn.

Endre Calder stands there for a moment in front of the bonfire, his hands resting on his hips. His skin is as pale as a pearl, long, silky white hair flying out behind his shoulders in the night breeze. He stands at about seven feet tall and weighs over three hundred pounds, all of it pure, rigid muscle, a body that looks like it was carved from ivory. His eyes are like scarlet orbs set into his head, eyes that immediately convey several things with a single glance. Power. Leadership. Cunning. Fantastic cruelty. Savagery unparalleled by any set of eyes Grady has ever looked into in his entire life.

Raymond once told Grady that Endre was born an albino. The snow white skin, the reddened eyes, the mane of bone-colored hair...all traits of the albinism.

He's the oldest of them. He's the shot caller. He's the one who runs the show.

"Ask and you shall receive, Raymond." Endre's voice seems to crawl up from the gravelly pit of his sternum, a deep, dark rasp. It's a voice that's oddly charming in its own way.

Raymond immediately casts his eyes back to the fire, an act of submission. Everyone here has a healthy mixture of fear and respect for Endre.

"Jok and Thon, would you be so kind as to liberate our guests from that poor excuse for a cell over there?"

The Twins immediately rise up, looking to Endre with something like reverence. They head straight for the van, both of them working to pull off a padlock and swing the barbwire door open. The young husband and wife are pulled from within, the wife whimpering and sobbing, the husband trying desperately to soothe her with words of hollow comfort.

The Twins force them to their knees near the bonfire, both man and woman kneeling there in the dirt amongst bits of broken bottles.

Endre steps a little closer, taking time to observe the couple.

"Jok, bring the young lady forward for a moment."

Jok complies, dragging the woman a little closer to Endre and the blazing fire. The husband protests weakly behind them before Thon pulls back on his hair and plants his other hand firmly across the man's mouth, his words turning to impotent mumbles.

The young wife kneels there before the massive albino, her pink top and bottoms coated in dust from the salvage yard. The boy watches from his place a few feet away. The woman was pulled from her bed last night. She's still in her pajamas...

"I know how deeply afraid you are right now. If your eyes were pools full of water, that water would be contaminated by fear. I can see it surging through your gaze. I know it's a difficult request, but I don't want you to feel so upset. I just want to talk to you, okay?"

Endre's voice is strangely disarming. The woman is still extremely unsettled, but she seems to try her best to compose herself as Endre kneels down in front of her so that they're eye to eye.

"Let's start with your name. What may I call you?" Endre asks, almost politely.

The woman attempts to reply, but she starts blubbering. Endre reaches out and places a gentle hand across her shoulder. She finally manages to string together a few words.

"My name is Anna. Please...we just had a son. A newborn son. Just let us go. Please just let Blake and I go..." She stops, Endre bringing a pallid finger to his lips in the classic "shh" gesture.

"It gives me no pleasure to keep you captive here. It's completely uncivilized. No one should be made to feel like a caged animal. Those feelings of restraint and confliction are poor substitutes for true freedom. Don't you think so, Anna?"

Endre makes brief eye contact with Grady when he says this. The boy finds his body trembling uncontrollably, but he tries very hard to hide it. Anna is nodding her head, the tears starting to dry on her cheeks.

"I am a perfectly reasonable man. I've lived a long, fulfilling life. I believe absolutely EVERYONE deserves a fair shot, Anna. America was founded on those same principles...this wild, untamed wilderness was made into a mecca devoted to opportunity."

Endre sighs, looking almost...nostalgic?

"I want to give you and your husband a fair and just opportunity. It's the chance for you to break your own chains, shake off your own shackles...and go live out the rest of your lives. The chance to kiss that newborn of yours on those little apple-bud cheeks and watch him grow into a strapping young man!"

Lizzie has lain down on her stomach on top of the corpse-hill, watching this unfold below with her chin draped in her hands. She occasionally picks at her chipped black nail polish as the drama unfolds. The Twins remain stoic, and Raymond just leers, something like a barely concealed grin pulling at his lips. The boy knows where this is going. The boy has seen it one too many times...

"All you have to do, Anna...is tell me where the people from that church are hiding. That is your golden ticket back to normal life."

Anna chokes back a sob, her eyes confused.

"What? I don't understand? Her voice quavers, a little bit of mucus starting to drip down from her left nostril. Endre remains incredibly patient, even smiling a little. His teeth look very white, very sharp.

"Last night you and your dear husband were fleeing with a few people towards that chapel on the west side of Old Hollow. We've located some of those people, but a few are missing. Where might they be hiding?"

Anna shakes her head from side to side, the tears dripping slowly down her cheeks. She bites her bottom lip hard.

"No lies, Anna. The truth sets you free. The truth lets you fly away..."

Anna's head drops. She seems to be thinking deeply, likely about her son. It's masterful manipulation on the part of Calder. The boy watches as it works just as flawlessly as Endre intended.

"There's a trap door. It's beneath a rug, under the pipe organ. They're down there. We all ran there...hoping to find sanctuary," she sobs, her throat working. "We almost made it but I twisted my ankle and Blake had to stop and help."

Endre rises back up to his feet, seeming satisfied.

"Thank you for being candid with me."

The boy watches as Anna's eyes fill up with hope.

"So you'll let us go?"

Endre casually removes a large serrated knife from his belt. He's shirtless, his scarred, pallid torso looking like something you'd see in a gladiatorial ludus. He sticks the blade into the flickering flames, allowing it to heat up.

"Just a moment," he says, watching carefully as the blade starts to take on a molten glow. "There's something I'd like you to suck on."

Anna's mouth falls agape, her eyes filling up with slow burning horror. Endre seems to pick up on this, a deep, hearty laugh booming up from his chest.

"Not my cock, silly goose! Just this."

In an eerily quick motion, Endre pivots on his heel and rams the heated blade into Anna's open mouth. There's a hideous gurgling sound as he digs the serrated blade around in her orifice, flesh and blood sizzling, a few tendrils of smoke creeping out past the woman's lips. He carves and twirls the knife until a lump of Anna's tongue falls out to plop down to the ground, all smoking, blackened meat. Lizzie giggles from her perch on the corpse-hill. Icy smiles form on the faces of The Twins at almost exactly the same time. Raymond seems to have an erection poking at his filthy jeans, and he casually rubs at it with one thumb.

Blake is moaning and reaching towards his wife, but The Twins easily hold him back. Endre finally withdraws the knife from Anna's mouth, her body in shock, her eyes gaping, a slow flood of boiled blood and flesh splattering out past her shredded lips. The albino then raises the blade up high and buries it up to the hilt in the top of Anna's head, proceeding to snap it to the side and break the handle clean off. The piercing of skull and brain takes less than a few seconds. Anna's body pitches forward, but Endre catches her by the hair.

He turns to the side and swings her around, tossing her at least ten feet over the fire, Anna's body landing in a heap on the top of the corpse-hill where Lizzie sits. Endre then turns to his brethren, shrugging his shoulders good naturedly.

"I said I'd let her fly away. Seems that little birdie flew pretty damn far..."

Raymond laughs his rotten laugh. The boy says nothing at all, a little desensitized to the graphic violence of what just occurred, but still internally disgusted by it. Lizzie pokes at Anna's corpse a few times before hopping downwards, using the corpse-hill like a slide you'd find at a playground.

Raymond motions to the husband, still struggling and crying in the firm arms of Jok and Thon.

"How about him?"

Endre seems to consider the question for a moment, the firelight dancing across his sharp, feral features.

"We'll string him up into a bait trap tomorrow. You all feel free to take his limbs, just make sure you cauterize the stumps when it's done. Bon appétit."

Endre stands there, his scarlet eyes seeming to stare straight into the depths of the bonfire. The Twins, Raymond, and Lizzie all descend upon the grieving husband. There are terrible ripping and snapping sounds, but that's not the worst. The worst is the chewing...the gnawing...the devouring.

Grady lies down on his bedroll and turns his back on it all.

9

Mallory

We put our heads together as best we can under the circumstances, and Asher comes up with an idea as day slowly turns to night. He thinks we should make a run for the library. It's not far from here, barely a few houses down and around the corner, but it's still risky. We don't know if the ones who did this are still out there, lurking and waiting, but staying here much longer just isn't an option. I was able to find some food and water stashed away in a few lunchboxes and thermoses in the station's little kitchenette, but it's almost all gone now, Cara nibbling on bits and pieces of a bologna sandwich all day. I'm glad she's getting her appetite back. My little girl is everything to me, and all that matters to me now is finding a way to pull her out of this waking nightmare.

Asher's idea is a good one. The library has multiple desktop computers and if they can gain access to the Internet, they can easily get help sent to town. It's the next best thing since the cell phones are dead and the landlines seem to have been cut. There's the lingering fear that something similar might have happened to the town's Internet access, but I can't allow myself to think that way. We can't be cut off completely. There *has* to be a way to contact the outside world and let them know that Old Hollow has been overrun by god knows what kind of depraved sickos.

I've only just met Asher, but I find myself warming to the man. He doesn't say much, but there's something about him that just exudes this quiet confidence. Even though he's not much for small talk, he seems to always be thinking, always some form of strategizing occurring within the deep wells of those slate-gray eyes. There are plenty of men in this town that talk big and seem to think everything can be accomplished with pissing contests and drunken brawls, and I'm glad it's not that sort of man that found us here. Asher is an island all his own, solitary and stoic, but I think him capable of getting us to that library in one piece. I hope I'm right. My daughter's future depends on it...

Asher managed to take up the shotgun Sergeant Wilks dropped before he died, even finding a cache of shells in the drawer of the scratched oaken desk. He hands the revolver off to me, his eyes meeting my own and holding them for a moment.

"Do you know how to use one of these?" he asks, his back to Sergeant Wilks, almost like he's deliberately blocking the corpse from view for Cara's benefit. She's clinging to my leg now, her little hands gripping desperately at the material of my slacks.

"My grandfather taught me to shoot when I was a teenager. I can manage."

He slips the revolver into my hand, the weight of it suddenly making all of this seem even more real. All three of us creep towards the door of the police station, Asher taking a moment to peek through the blinds, his eyes darting from left to right.

"The streets look clear. A few of the buildings are still smoking and sending up embers, but I don't see any movement."

Asher points his finger through the blinds. All I can see in that direction is a partially burnt townhouse and stranger still, a pile of satellite dishes that appear to have been ripped from the roofs of several homes and piled up on the sidewalk. A few of the streetlamps are still working, and the stars shine extra bright tonight, adding to the illumination.

"The library is just around that bend. We stay low and we keep our eyes open. If we see anyone that means to do us harm, don't hesitate to fire your weapon."

Cara tugs on my pant's leg, her eyes huge and afraid.

"But mommy, the red paint on the wall says that bullets don't stop them…"

A shiver travels down my spine as I pull Cara's head closer to my leg. That cryptic message on the wall seems to unsettle me most of all, even more than the sight of those smoking homes and ruined streets beyond the window.

"Don't look at that, honey. Don't even think about that."

Asher looks down at the little girl, one heavy hand reaching out to push a strand of hair out of her eyes.

"Stay close to your mom. There are lots of storybooks at the library. Stories about knights and princesses and big, beautiful castles. Do you like stories, Cara?"

Cara nods, sniffling. Asher leans down to her, smiling gently. The starlight drifts in through the blinds, catching in Cara's golden hair and Asher's thick, black beard.

"What about monsters? Will the knights fight the monsters?" Cara asks, her face so innocent, so perfectly naïve. Asher stands back up, an amused grin dawning across his lips. He can't help but chuckle.

"Always, Cara. That's what knights are born to do..."

He makes eye contact with me now, a subtle nod exchanged between us. I hold tight to Cara's hand, my other hand slick with sweat as I grip the revolver. Nothing remains to be said. All that's left is action...and whatever waits for us beyond this door.

Asher opens it as silently as he can, the hinges creaking ever so slightly as the night pours in.

10

Asher

I hold tight to the twelve gauge as I lead Mallory and Cara across the street, my eyes darting from left to right, trying to look everywhere at once. The streets are abnormally quiet. A few tattered papers float on the breeze from several of the burnt shells that used to be homes, but that's the only movement I notice out here.

I make a motion to Mallory for us to stop and crouch next to the pile of battered satellite dishes. I very carefully peek around the detritus, checking Cobalt Street for any sign of danger. In the distance there's a broken fire hydrant still sending up a few bursts of slow, sluggish water...but that seems to be all. The steps leading up to the library look deserted. The whole town seems to have taken on that same atmosphere, absolute desertion. I know better though. Something waits in all this silence. The ones responsible for this are still out there, just biding time. I can feel that in the actual air I breathe, almost like the oxygen of Old Hollow has been tainted by the iron-scent of far too much spilled blood. Blood spilled recently and in a variety of atrocious ways...

I motion with two fingers that we should keep moving, and Mallory nods at my side. I have to give Cara credit, the little girl is being incredibly brave and quiet, her big eyes the only indicator of how deeply terrified she is right now. We begin moving down Cobalt Street, keeping as low as possible, even using the hedges near the library entrance for cover. We carefully duck the railing and climb up onto the stairs, both Mallory and I helping to lift Cara.

You read a lot when you live alone in the mountains. Sometimes you have nothing but time, and reading helps me fill the hours. Based on a few helpful nonfiction books, I've managed to become a fairly proficient lock picker. My great hope is that the main entrance doors aren't locked though, because if I'm crouched down working at the keyhole, that's going to leave us exposed for longer than I'm comfortable with.

It seems fate smiles upon us this time, because the door swings open easily, no sign of resistance at all.

I usher Mallory and Cara into the library's lobby first, and then I turn to shut the door tight behind us. The library is a two story building—I should know, I've been here enough times—and a spiral staircase leads up to the little office area where the community PCs are kept. We start towards that staircase, passing by the large circular front desk where Luther the Librarian can usually be found. I always liked Luther, the old man a seemingly bottomless well of knowledge when it comes to all things books. He's one of the few people in Old Hollow that I would actually consider a friend. There's no sign of Luther in his familiar spot now, and I can only hope he made it out of this mess in one piece.

We're closing in on the bottom of the staircase when a loud, wet explosion freezes all three of us firmly in place. Cara just sneezed, her little arm already reaching up to wipe at her nose. I'm just about to reach for the tissue box on the front desk when a huge metal door swings open behind the desk and a burly man with a crew cut and a camouflaged shirt comes lunging out of it, a crowbar raised up high in his hand and baleful intentions in his eyes. I'm already pushing Mallory and Cara behind me, the attacker closing the distance between us, my arms bringing the shotgun up and centering the barrel on the attacker's chest. A loud yell from behind the thick door stops us both.

"NO, VIC! I know that man. He's not one of *them*."

All of the motion stops at once, the man in the camouflaged shirt stopping in his tracks with the crowbar still held tentatively in his right hand. My finger eases away from the shotgun's trigger. I immediately recognize the kind, soft-spoken voice that came from beyond the metal door. It's a diplomatic voice with the power to hold violence at bay...

Luther steps out a moment later, the old man looking bright-eyed in the glow of the library's dome lighting. His silver hair is tied back into a loose ponytail, the wrinkles around his mouth stretching as he smiles at me.

"Good to see you, Asher," he says, that warm smile seeming to put everyone at ease, even the mercurial man he identified as Vic. "Come to return your library books?"

I can't help but grin in return. I pat the leather satchel that hangs from my shoulder.

"I've got them right here, Luther. Thanks for recommending Bukowski. I loved his stuff."

Luther laughs heartily, his voice full of energy for a man who has to be at least in his mid to late seventies.

"Even with hellfire and madness tearing Old Hollow apart, you still manage to return your library books on time. You're a credit to the human species, my dear boy."

Luther casts his eyes to the main entrance, a wary glimmer taking shape behind his gold-rimmed spectacles. The old man nods towards the large metal door he just emerged from.

"It's not safe out here. How about we continue our little chat behind a steel-enforced vault door? One of the few perks left over from the old days when this library was converted from a bank...and it's served Vic and I well so far."

I immediately nod my assent. The computers upstairs can wait. Maybe Luther has some more information about what's happening out there, and my main priority right now is getting Mallory and Cara somewhere out of harm's way.

We all follow Luther through the circular opening, and I put my back into helping the old man close the heavy vault door behind us.

***

What once was a secure bank vault many decades ago has now been refurbished into something like a library within the library, a secret holdout lined with many shelves on all sides, the space sectioned off into two separate rooms. It seems Luther has designated one of the rooms as a temporary "living area", sleeping bags laid out on the floor and a small refrigerator stocked with bottled water and a few sealed edibles. The other room is lined from wall to wall with bookshelves, a rolling ladder set up against one of the shelves and a few stools and a table set up in the center of the room.

Luther gestures to the table, and Mallory and I take seats, Luther himself moving over to the stool closest to a lamplit corner. The dim glow of the lamp shows every wrinkle on the weathered valley of his face, but Luther has young eyes, the youngest eyes I've ever seen. They seem almost to sparkle, a deep shade of hazel that defies his elderly countenance. Only Vic doesn't sit, the man leaning with his arms crossed against one of the shelves, looking vaguely sullen.

"This place proved very convenient when the bad times started. We keep the valuable books back here, first editions, rare tomes, things of that nature. It's practically a fortress, so don't worry about *them* for now." Luther's voice has a calming effect, even Cara seeming to relax a bit, the fear taking a backseat to exhaustion for the time being.

"We came here to try the computers, Luther. Is there still Internet access?"

The old librarian sighs, his head slowly shaking. I notice that a light fuzz of gray stubble has started to appear on his chin, likely due to not being able to shave given the recent circumstances.

"I'm afraid not. We lost Internet access right after the...first wave; I guess you'd call it? It went right along with the cell phone signals and the cut landlines. I can quote Hemingway verbatim and tell you all about the life and struggles of Oscar Wilde, but I can't say I'm a very tech savvy fellow. All I can tell you is that there's no Wi-Fi left in town, and as you know the only major Internet service provider in Old Hollow is the satellite option. It seems *they* have torn the very dishes down from the rooftops and destroyed them," Luther pauses, taking a moment to adjust his glasses. "Certain sections of town are without electricity as well, mostly on the far west side. It seems the goal was a total communication breakdown, essentially cutting us off completely."

I try my best to hide my frustration, but a muttered "damn it" still escapes my lips. Whoever these bastards are, they're smart...and it seems like they've done this kind of thing before.

"What do you know about these people, Luther?" I lean forward on my stool, all of my attention focused on the old man.

I might not be the best talker around, but I'd rank myself very high on the listener scale.

"Very little, my friend. They came like wraiths in the night, burning homes, shooting and hacking at townsfolk...it was just...a systematic slaughter," Luther's voice wavers, the emotion bubbling through. "They seem to thrive on carnage, just absolute savagery. I was working late in the archive section and Vic was mopping in the lobby. He's the janitor, works the graveyard shift."

Vic says nothing, just continuing to lean back against the shelves, his eyes hard and his mouth closed in a tight line.

"Vic and I watched from behind the blinds. They killed like it was *nothing* to them. Anyone that put up any kind of resistance—and there were a few—paid for it in literal pounds of their own flesh. It seemed the whole world was on fire beyond that window. It looked as though the ground had opened up and the depths of Tartarus had spat these abominations out like a plague of locusts."

Mallory speaks up now, trying her best to soothe Cara by rubbing at the little girl's shoulders and the back of her neck.

"Do you know how many of them there are?

Luther takes a moment to think, his head lowering.

"I only counted three from the window...but I believe there are more. I saw one not much younger than myself, dirty and decrepit, his beard reaching down to his chest. He went from home to home with a torch and some flammable liquid, setting them all ablaze and driving the occupants out. Two walked along behind him, a tall black man and a woman with her hair shaved on one side and twisting serpents tattooed along her arms. The houses would burn, the people that lived inside of them would run out screaming...and the tall man and the woman would run them down and just tear them apart. There's no other way to describe the deaths. I saw it only from a distance...but those poor souls were literally just ripped to shreds right there in the middle of the road."

Luther's words wash over me, his explanation painting such a vivid picture of that night in my head. Even just imagining it I see nothing but a nightmare world smeared in gore and hopelessness.

"There was something else, Asher. Something...especially peculiar. I've been thinking about it, turning it round and round in my mind, but I can't see the meaning in it. After each house the bearded one set the torch to, he would then...urinate on the doorstep. At first I thought the old man just had a weak bladder—I can sympathize at my age—but he kept doing it...with every single house. But what stays with me most of all is after the woman had just torn into a man's chest with her bare hands, she pulled her pants down and did the exact same thing," Luther's eyes shimmer with confusion, one hand reaching up to rub his temple. "She stood right there in the middle of the road...and she pissed on the man's corpse."

Thankfully Mallory has placed her hands over Cara's ears for most of this, trying to keep the little girl ignorant to the gritty details. Luther stares at me now, almost like he hopes I might have an answer to this bizarre puzzle.

"Why would they do that, Asher? Just desecration to follow the destruction?"

I don't answer for quite awhile, my own mind working over the problem.

"I guess that's possible...but what you just described? Animals do that. It's called scent marking. They do it to mark their territory."

A heavy silence hangs over the room, the tension like a live wire that's whipping from side to side. Luther finally breaks the spell.

"But these were people doing it. Why would people...behave like wild animals?"

Luther's question remains unanswered, dreadful thoughts infecting the room.

***

Vic finally joins the conversation, his voice a low, gruff timbre. He casts his eyes on Luther and runs one hand over his shaved head, scrubbing at the stubble there in a gesture of frustration.

"Here we go with this crap, Luther. Please don't tell me you're gonna start in about those *dark shapes* again."

Mallory cocks her head to the side, suddenly curious.

"Dark shapes? What's he talking about?" she asks, her golden mane of hair seeming to brighten up the grim little room, giving it just a modicum of beauty in an otherwise desperate situation.

"Vic likes to wave his hands and call me an old fool, but I know what I saw. I stood at that window for quite awhile, even after Vic got tired of looking and went to try and phone the police. It was bright out there, the streetlamps shining and the moon casting light over just about everything. Soon the people responsible for torching the houses and murdering the occupants moved along. I lost sight of them. I started to see just regular townsfolk emerging from here and there, crowding around in the road and talking to each other, trying to make sense of all this," Luther hesitates, but Mallory nods her head, urging him on. "That's when the dark shapes came...and started picking them off, dragging them into alleys, crevices, behind parked cars. It all happened so fast, I never got a chance to see what the *things* actually were. They loped through the streets in mere seconds, keeping to the shadows, dragging men, women, even children out of the road. When my view from the window was barren, all that remained was the screaming. It seemed to come from all over town, west, east, north, and south...just an orchestra of suffering, all those gurgling screams mixing together to create some wretched, ravaged music."

Luther seems overcome by the retelling of this for a moment, his head lowering as he takes his head into his hands.

"It made me want to drive sharpened pencils into my own eardrums. So many screams. So much unified pain. It was like the entire town of Old Hollow was baying in misery, seeking some kind of reprieve from those huge, horrible shapes..."

Luther turns his gaze to make eye contact with me before turning to look at Mallory as well. I've never seen such conviction in the librarian's eyes before.

"Those shapes were not human beings. I tell you that now with the utmost sincerity. I don't have the slightest idea what they were, but they were *not* human beings."

Vic groans loudly, proceeding to pace back and forth near the shelves.

"No disrespect to this old-timer here, but he's been blathering on about that damn nonsense ever since we've been holed up in this vault. I'm tired of hearing that hocus pocus bullshit, and we sure as hell ain't dealing with no damn ghosts and goblins out in the streets. This is serious business going on. If you'd pull that nose outta all these damn books and watch the television once and awhile—like normal folk do—you'd clearly see what's happened to this town."

Vic approaches the table, laying his palms on top of it while passing his stare to each and every one of us. He has hard, stubborn eyes. They're the eyes of a man who likes to throw his weight around. I've seen his type way too many times before.

"It's been all over the news lately. What's happened is a full-scale motherfuckin' terrorist attack! It could be ISIS, or could be some other group of whacky jihadists looking to take out some decent blue-collar folk. And if it ain't that? Well, hell...you never know. Could be some of those high school kids got bullied or somethin' and decided to pick up some rifles and go shooting up people and burning up houses. Ain't y'all ever heard of Columbine before?"

Vic nods his head hard and fast, acting as though everyone agrees with him even though none of us have responded yet. Luther can only sigh.

"Vic and I have discussed this theory quite a bit prior to your arrival, and as you've probably guessed, we just can't agree. Why would terrorists choose Old Hollow, Vic? This is an isolated mountain town in the middle of nowhere with a population below the 200 range. There are no national monuments here. This isn't some big city that would cause a media firestorm if ISIS attacked. It just doesn't add up."

I can't help but chime in now, my thoughts whirling through my head and gaining steam.

"I have to agree with Luther, Vic. I considered terrorists too when I first got into town...but something in my gut tells me that isn't the case here. And it seems many of us at this table have actually seen some of the people responsible for this. They're not high school kids on some kind of revenge mission. These people are strangers. No one has seen them in Old Hollow prior to what happened last night..."

Vic bristles, throwing his hands up in the air and walking away from the table to lean up against the shelves again.

"What in the blue fuck do y'all think is going on out there then?" he asks, his voice rising just a bit, sounding especially self-righteous.

"I think we don't have enough information right now to form an accurate hypothesis about who these people are or what they want in Old Hollow. Here's what I do know. The phones are dead. The computers are useless. If we can't call for help, that leaves us only one option right now. We need to get out of town. The only road leading out of Old Hollow is Route 56...and we need to follow it and get to safety while things are still relatively quiet."

Vic seems to actually get behind this idea, immediately digging into his pocket for his keys.

"I'm all for that. Uhh...Asher, was it? My van is parked out back. I say we all pile into it right now and haul ass for Inwood."

I shake my head, wishing deep down that it was that easy.

"No vehicles, Vic. We start an engine and they'll hear it...and then they'll come for us. We're gonna have to go on foot, and we're gonna have to go quietly. Wilderness borders Route 56 on both sides as soon as we get beyond the town limits. We can head into the trees and follow the road from there."

"Are you shitting me, boy? Inwood is 120 miles from here! Nothing between here and there but woods and more woods. You wanna hoof it all that way?"

"I don't see any other viable options right now. There's nothing behind us but North Mountain, the best course is to go south and head towards Inwood. It's the only other town even vaguely close to here. If we're lucky we'll run into a car on Route 56 on the way to Inwood..."

Everyone at the table seems to mull this over. Mallory is the first to speak up, Cara looking around the room while sucking on the tip of her thumb.

"I think Asher is right. We can't risk drawing them out by making noise with a car. We walk, we stay hidden and we stay quiet...we get clear of this nightmare."

"There's really nothing else to be done. We can't hide forever here." says Luther, a firm determination settling across the wrinkled canvas of the old man's face.

All eyes seem to fall on Vic at once. His teeth are gritted as though he means to put up some kind of resistance, but finally he relents.

"I think our feet are gonna be mighty goddamn sore after we start out on that road, but if it gets us outta this clusterfuck of a situation, then I guess it's as good a plan as any."

That seems to settle the matter. There's some more discussion, and provisions from the fridge are added into my satchel and Mallory's large purse. We should have enough food and bottled water for the trip. Luther even packs a few books, a first edition of Bram Stoker's Dracula, a tattered first edition of The Prophecies by Nostradamus, and even a 16th century untitled grimoire bound in pure silver, the script within etched in Latin. Vic shakes his head at the old man bringing books, telling him they'll just weigh him down, but Luther seems steadfast about bringing the priceless volumes along. The plan is to get a good night's rest and set out for Route 56 in the morning.

The trip to Inwood on foot could take as long as four days, but we hope to meet a car on the road before then. If it comes down to it we plan to camp in the wilderness on the side of the road. The weather's still warm so a few nights sleeping beneath the stars might be uncomfortable, but not debilitating.

It's the best shot we have right now. I'm hoping in the deepest part of myself that it pays off...

11

Salvage Yard (Den)

It's hard for Grady to look at what remains of Blake, the unfortunate husband, the freshly maimed prisoner. The boy tries to avert his eyes as he spoons cooked meat into Blake's mouth, his lips chapped and dripping with slobber. The boy makes the mistake of meeting Blake's eyes directly as he sucks listlessly on the spoon. Those eyes are hopeless, utterly lost. They're the eyes of a man who realizes that he is far beyond broken.

"A few more spoonfuls, Grady. We have to keep this piglet healthy for a little while longer. He'll soon play a pivotal role..."

Endre's voice is like icy fingers caressing the back of Grady's neck, the flames of the bonfire painting the albino with harsh, infernal light. He sits on a tattered leather chair that was torn from a charter bus, the seat resting on a few wooden pallets and concrete blocks. He's currently using a shard of human femur as a toothpick. The boy can't help but think of it as a throne for a pallid king, Endre lounging there with Lizzie curled up in his lap and practically purring.

The corpse-hill looms overtop of all of them in their little circle around the bonfire. It's even bigger now, becoming like an Everest of torn, brutalized bodies. It's even attracted buzzards, the carrion birds circling endlessly above the salvage yard, casting winged shadows over Endre and his brethren.

Raymond is busy stripping the clothes from a few newly arrived corpses, tossing the garments into the fire, sending up crackling sparks now and again. Grady finally steps back from Blake, his head hanging low—a low that matches his spirits.

The Twins step forward now, both of them taking turns with their notepad. Their eyes dart from paper to Blake, totally unsympathetic, just cold, obsidian orbs set within their skulls.

Jok tears a sheet of paper loose and holds it out to Blake, his sick, rolling eyes taking in the words there. Thon tears off another sheet, showing it to those same bedeviled eyes.

"My brother is showing you your script for tomorrow. It's very simple, only a few words. Memorize it."

Jok continues to hold the sheet up, allowing Blake to stare at it for awhile. Thon flips his sheet around, Blake's eyes taking in the words written there.

"If you deviate from the script, you suffer."

Grins appear on the faces of The Twins at the exact same moment, slivers of white teeth in dark, detached faces. They stare down at Blake's pitiful form, seeming to enjoy just looking at it, almost like they're appreciating the artistry of his ruined body. Blake is nothing more than a torso now. His arms were amputated below the elbows, his legs below the knees. The wounds were immediately cauterized, the stumps looking inflamed and charred. His head lolls from side to side, fat crocodile tears dripping down his ruddy cheeks.

"He reminds me of a chicken nugget," says Lizzie, a wicked little giggle sliding from her mouth as Endre rises from his throne, slowly walking over towards what is left of Blake's body. The rest of the group remains silent as Endre approaches, The Twins stepping back to give him access. Even Raymond stops his work with the fresh corpses, the old bastard crouching there and watching the albino with attentive eyes. Grady keeps to the shadows, trying to stay out of Endre's way.

The albino leans over Blake, white hair hanging down to frame his vulpine features. Those scarlet eyes seem to burn just as bright as the bonfire itself, almost competing with the flames.

"Poor guy. Look at you. Reduced to nothing but stumps and teardrops. It's a cold, hard world, isn't it, Blake?"

Blake's streaming eyes fall to Endre's lower body, sizing up the antique six shooter that Endre has tucked beneath the leather of his belt. He starts blubbering, even waving one of his severed stumps in the direction of the gun.

"Please shoot me. Please. Kill me. Just please...I'm begging you..."

His words die away as a stream of messy saliva drips out of his mouth to mingle with the snot pouring from his nose. Endre grins, his teeth far too sharp, making a little "tsk tsk" gesture with one hand.

"Sorry, pal. Not an option for you. And besides, these guns, knives, hatchets...even the torches? They're mostly just for theatricality. We don't necessarily even need them. We have...natural gifts."

Endre chuckles, Raymond and Lizzie laughing right along with him while the mute Twins simply grin those barren grins.

"I just find it easier to flush you little piggies out with flames and gunfire. It always works like a charm. Trust me; I'm experienced in these matters. Plus it adds to the fun!"

Blake is sobbing now, just silent, broken sobbing. Grady is finding this harder and harder to watch with each passing moment. Endre reaches out and forcefully grabs the man's shoulders so that Blake has no choice but to make eye contact with him.

"You have work to do tomorrow, my nugget servant. Your new career...is live bait. I'm going to place you in a car outside of that chapel, and I'm going to drape a nice big poncho over you so that no one notices that you're now just a limbless torso. You're going take one of your new stumps and lay on that horn, and you're gonna yell out the words on that script that Jok showed you as loud as you possibly can. Until your lungs burst, if that's what it takes."

Endre rises back up to his full height, his mammoth shadow falling over Blake. The poor man's body has been placed on a filthy mattress and propped up next to a rusted factory machine. The mattress is already soaked in Blake's urine.

"Now best case scenario, your friends come running out of their little hidey-hole beneath that chapel with hope in their hearts...and my friends come out to meet them and massacre them. Sound like a plan?"

Blake is shaking his head from side to side, parts of his skull bashing up against the rusted machine he's leaned up against.

"You have the right to refuse me, Blake. It's a free country. Here's what happens if you do. First, I use my fingernails to carve out your eyeballs. That leaves you limbless *and* sightless. I'll then toss your eyeballs over to Lizzie and you can listen to her eat them."

Lizzie has risen up to her knees on the old bus seat, clapping her hands together in excitement. Her turquoise eyes swirl with depravity, her tongue slipping out to lap at ruby-painted lips.

Lizzie had her tongue forked at a tattoo parlor a few years back, so it makes the visual even more repugnant.

"They're my favorite. They taste kinda like grape jelly."

Raymond snorts with laughter, a sadistic hunger flickering in the old man's eyes.

"I know they are, sugar tits. And you'll have them if our boy Blake here doesn't cooperate. Secondly, Blake...and this might hit just a little closer to home if you've stopped caring about your own personal wellbeing. Before I murdered your wife, it was mentioned that you two just had a newborn son, right? I believe the little bundle of joy is staying at your parent's house a few towns over..."

Finally something other than despair awakens in Blake's eyes. He strains his neck up, his face beet-red with a mixture of impotent rage and horror.

"Don't you hurt my son. Don't you dare hurt my little boy..."

The albino throws up his hands, his facial expression contorting into something that resembles faux-innocence.

"I wouldn't dream of it, Blake! As long as you do as you're told tomorrow. But...if you get any rebellious ideas? I'm going to hunt that newborn down. I'm going to huff, and puff, and blow your parent's house down..."

Endre leans closer to Blake's face now, their noses almost touching. Endre's grin is larger than ever, a mouth full of toothy razorblades.

"And then I'm gonna pop that newborn into my mouth and chew him up like a kidney bean. Do we have an understanding?"

The tears are leaking fresh now; Blake forcing his head up and down in assent.

"I'll do what you want. Just don't hurt my baby."

Endre clasps his hands together, looking extremely satisfied. He heads back to his throne, getting comfortable once again and allowing Lizzie to slither across his lap.

"Fan-fuckin-tastic. That's all I needed to hear. You deliver an award-winning performance tomorrow and you have nothing to *worry* about. I'll even give you that bullet you asked for after it's done. I'll put it into your brain myself."

Blake seems to fall into the silent nothingness of his own depression now, the torso that was once a man just slumping back against his saturated mattress.

"Grady, a few more spoonfuls before he goes to bed. He's looking a little weak. We only need him to last one more day. We need that voice to roar out loud and proud for those good-hearted church folk!"

The boy creeps forward out of the shadows, taking up the spoon again and reluctantly dipping it into the stew pot that simmers above the bonfire. He starts feeding Blake again, hating himself more and more as he does it, the man's eyes simply listless and lost at this point.

Grady's one merciful wish is for Blake to never realize that he's being kept alive on bits and pieces of his own severed arms and legs.

12

Mallory

Cara is curled up in her blanket, her thumb gently tucked between her lips. I'm not surprised she fell asleep so quickly, this entire ordeal has just exhausted her completely. It takes a lot to deplete the energy reserves of a little girl her age, but the hell we've been through since "that night" seems to have done the trick.

My body craves rest, but my mind just won't turn off. I keep thinking about tomorrow and all the possible scenarios we could run into. I don't think of myself as pessimistic, but I can't help but let the negative ideas swim around in my head. What happens if we don't make it out of town? What (or who) could we run into on the way? It just seems that there are so many things that could go wrong...

Finally I rise up from my sleeping bag, making sure to tuck Cara in a little better. Luther and Vic are just dark shapes in their own sleeping bags, Vic's snores rumbling out of him like mini-bursts of thunder. I don't see Asher's shape. I assume he's sleeping in the next room with the bookshelves.

I head there now, keeping my footsteps light. I'm thinking of trying to pull down something to read for awhile until my body finally allows me to sleep. I can't say I'm greatly surprised to see Asher sitting up in his sleeping bag in one corner, the glow from the lamp shining down on an open book in his hands.

I just watch him for a moment, taking in the man who is largely responsible for getting us all on the same page with this escape plan. I don't think he even realizes he's become the de facto leader of this little ragtag band of townsfolk. I doubt a private man like him would even want such a role...

His black hair is combed back from his brow, his beard neatly trimmed and cared for. He doesn't strike me as fitting the typical hermit archetype. He's not a dirty, disheveled kook running around draped in animal furs and a coonskin cap.

He seems almost to draw strength from his solitude, even isolating himself from the others slumbering in the next room. It doesn't strike me as something he does to ostracize himself from us; it just seems like something he *needs*. The opportunity to recharge his batteries, to be alone with himself and his thoughts.

I clear my throat just a little, stepping into the room. He looks up from his book, his eyes sparkling with a certain empathetic gleam. He gestures to the spot beside him on the floor. I take it, hunkering down next to him.

"Guess you couldn't sleep either, huh?" I ask, my voice lowered to a whisper.

He shakes his head, taking a moment to mark his page in the book before closing it.

"You guessed right."

A silence follows. It's a comfortable silence; neither of us feeling obligated to say anything for a moment or so. It feels good to just sit here, momentarily aware that we're safe from whatever threat still lurks outside.

"Can I ask you something?"

He turns to me, giving me his full attention.

"Sure."

I pause a moment, thinking of the best way to phrase the question. I can feel the lightest blush rushing into my cheeks and I do my best to let it fade.

"Why do you live on that mountain all by yourself?"

Now Asher is the one who seems to pause. He takes his time with the question, his face looking contemplative.

"I like the quiet, Mallory. Living up there is hard, but it's also simple. The hard part is scratching out a living from the land. The simple part is being absolutely free. Free to listen to the crickets at twilight. Free to watch the deer foraging on the ridges just as dawn breaks. Free from people, and all the drama and turmoil that tends to come with them..."

I watch his face closely. I can see it in his eyes, that longing for his mountain, his private serenity.

"Do you ever get lonely up there?"

"There are times when I do. That's the great sacrifice when you decide to live off the grid. Sometimes I wake up in my cabin and I feel like I'm the last man on earth. Other times I wake up and think about just how lucky I am..."

Asher shrugs, smiling. His smile lights up features that could be mistaken for dark and aloof.

"There's so much beauty up there, indescribable beauty. I'm not built for the rat race, the 9 to 5 grind...it's a cage I just can't willingly walk into. I don't miss society as a whole. There's too much ugliness in society, too many petty quarrels."

Asher runs his hardened hands over the surface of the hardcover in his hands, tracing the title.

"I'm only lonely when I realize I don't have anyone up there to share all that beauty with. It makes me feel selfish in a way, hoarding it all up for myself. That probably sounds stupid."

He smiles again, his eyes falling downward. I've never met a man quite like this one. There's something tragic about him, a flawed gentleness behind his resolve. It endears him to me. It makes me come to the sudden realization that I'm attracted to this man, this loner from the hills that I've barely just met...

"It doesn't sound stupid. It sounds honest. There's not enough honesty left in the world these days..."

That silence comes again, embracing us, blanketing us, making me feel warmth in my heart. My hand reaches over to touch the cover of his book, our fingers touching for the briefest of moments.

"What are you reading?"

"Frankenstein by Mary Shelley. I'm envious of Luther's copy..."

Now it's my turn to smile, a few locks of hair falling down to brush against my cheek.

"A classic. I've never read the book, though. Does it have a happy ending?"

Asher meets my gaze, so much soul in his eyes, soul that seems to have no bottom.

"Not quite. The ending isn't happy...but it's the right ending."

He pauses, choosing his words carefully.

"Some stories tell themselves, and this one leads to the right ending. The only ending it ever could have had."

This time the silence lasts longer.

I hope our story has the right ending.

Most of all though, I hope we manage to squeeze a little happiness out of it along the way...

13

Asher

We leave the next morning, each of us carrying makeshift packs filled with water and food. I have the shotgun, Mallory keeps the revolver, and Vic clings tight to his trusty crowbar. Luther caresses his heavy bag of books, holding them across his chest almost like some talisman to ward off evil.

We're careful while stepping down the library's outer staircase, all of us forming a rudimentary circle around Cara when we move. The little girl has a SpongeBob coloring book rolled up in her tiny hands, her eyes seeming to look everywhere at once. Nothing moves on Cobalt Street. Most of the burnt homes are just piles of ash and rubble now, even the smoke dissipating as the wind picks up.

A few sparrows chirp overhead and all of us tense up at the sound, our feet stealthily carrying us back towards Main Street. Hearing those birds singing reminds me that there's still normalcy left in the world, and if we make it out of town, that normalcy will return to our lives. That thought keeps me going. Mallory's golden hair twirling in the breeze keeps me going. Luther's love for his books keeps me going. The preservation of Cara's innocence keeps me going. Even Vic's hardboiled demeanor keeps my boots moving across the ground. I don't understand exactly why, but I feel responsible for these people. I keep thinking of them as "my" people. I associate that word "my" with them...realizing that this little group of human beings might very well be the last ones left alive in Old Hollow. I have to get them out to Route 56. I have to safeguard what is left of this town's shattered humanity...

We keep low past the trees, occasionally locking our eyes on porches and narrow alleyways to ensure that no threat is present. We're approaching the hill now, still going south. At the crest of that hill Main Street becomes Route 56. Vic and I make it over the hill first, a muttered "shit" escaping Vic's lips.

We can see it even from half a mile away. Someone has blocked off the only road out of town with an eighteen wheeler, the tractor trailer's rear and back end wedged up against the sharp granite cliffs that border Old Hollow's one and only entrance—and exit.

It becomes immediately clear that no traffic will be coming into town or going out of town with that mammoth truck stretched across the road.

"We're fucked," Vic groans, his hands falling to his hips.

I stare a little longer at the truck, my eyes assessing the makeshift roadblock from afar. If there's one gift I've always had, it's crystal clear vision. It's always helped when hunting game on North Mountain and it helps me locate the roadblock's weaknesses now.

"Not necessarily. No vehicles are getting past that, but if a few people on foot are motivated enough, we can manage it. We'll need to either crawl under...or find a way to climb over."

We keep on moving, the others gathered around as we mull this over, thinking of the best way to overcome the obstacle that we're faced with. We're passing Meridian Drive now, nothing much down there on the west end of town but Old Hollow's chapel and a few mobile homes.

We suddenly all freeze in place in the middle of the road. There's a sound ringing in our ears, our eyes all falling towards Meridian Drive at the same time. It's the blaring of a car horn.

The honking just goes on and on, seeming to originate from an old station wagon parked near the church's entrance...

***

"What the hell is that?" asks Vic, his mouth pulled down into a confused grimace.

Vic and Luther are already starting towards the station wagon, and I'm quick to step forward and pull them both back.

"Wait. Something doesn't feel right..."

I can't really describe it, but my instincts are telling me the sound of that horn spells trouble. I don't know what kind of trouble, but I can't shake the sour stirring in my stomach. Something just seems slightly off. I motion the others back towards a tall wooden fence with a few cracks between the boards, the fence separating one house with broken windows from another with a partially charred garage.

"First we wait...and we watch."

I climb over the fence, reaching over for Mallory to hand me Cara so that I'm able to get the little girl over too. The others reluctantly follow, crouching down behind the fence and obscured from the view of anyone who might be in that station wagon.

"It might be someone that needs help," says Luther, his eyes looking conflicted behind his glasses.

"It might also be *them*," answers Mallory, her hands wrapped protectively around her daughter. We all peek through the cracks in the fence, watching the station wagon as the horn keeps right on honking. I barely see the form of a man behind the wheel, the windows of the vehicle extremely dusty and not offering up much of a view.

"We give it a few minutes...then we'll check it out."

I can't really explain my logic for offering the others this reply. It's just something I feel in my blood, a heaviness hanging over Meridian Drive and the station wagon itself. The vehicle looks so grimy and battered, like something you'd find in a used car lot that sells only lemons...or even at a salvage yard.

But still, that heaviness remains. So much tension entrapped in the blaring of a car horn...

14

Live Bait

Finally the horn stops, replaced by yelling from the open driver's side window of the station wagon. The voice carries across Meridian Drive, words slipping through the cracks of the chapel's doors.

"PASTOR WHITMAN! IT'S BLAKE ALLAN. IT'S SAFE NOW...THE ONES THAT DID THIS HAVE LEFT TOWN!"

There's the briefest pause before the voice bellows again, tinged with exhaustion and weakness.

"BRING YOUR PEOPLE OUT...I'LL DRIVE US OUT OF HERE."

A long, pregnant silence follows this, no movement at all from the church. Finally after what seems like a very long time, the heavy oaken doors creak open just a few inches. A wizened face peers out, taking in the station wagon. The eyes peering out from that face immediately recognize Blake Allan sitting behind the wheel.

The door swings open even wider, several others crowding behind the man with the white clerical collar wrapped around his neck. Pastor Whitman takes a cautious step away from the doors, now fully recognizing Blake's features.

"Oh Blake, our prayers are answered..."

The priest motions to what remains of his congregation, around ten people following behind Pastor Whitman, all of them looking fearful and harrowed by this ordeal. There are around six men and four women, a few of them elderly while the great majority would fall within the middle-aged bracket.

Pastor Whitman makes a beeline for the station wagon, placing both hands across the vehicle's rusty rooftop as he looks in at Blake. Blake looks incredibly sickly, his eyes red-rimmed...absolutely haunted. A dark poncho is draped over his body despite the heat of the day, nothing visible but that pallid face and those staring, vacant eyes.

"Are you well, my friend? Where's Anna?"

Blake just stares at Pastor Whitman for a few moments. He can't hold back the tears any longer, shame eating up his face, twisting and contorting the features. He leans his head slightly out the window just as a portion of the poncho slides from his side, exposing the raw, infected stump where his right hand should be. He whispers up into the priest's face, a few droplets of spittle oozing down past his badly chapped lips.

"Forgive me."

The whisper hangs there in the air, a prelude, the final utterance before skulking devils rise up all around Pastor Whitman and his little tattered congregation.

Raymond springs up to his feet from beneath a mound of black plastic garbage bags, trash flying all around him, a few tendrils of garbage juice dripping down to decorate his straggly beard. The Twins slither out from underneath a mobile home, twisting like dark serpents with dead leaves clinging to their gangly bodies. Lizzie flips down from the limbs of a birch tree, landing with perfect grace, her scuffed combat boots meeting the asphalt. The Pastor spins in a slow panorama, realizing his terrible mistake...and that's when the doors of the tin shed across the street explode outward, the massive pale giant stepping out to stand beneath the sunlight, every scar showing on his exposed alabaster chest.

The albino greets Pastor Whitman with a winning smile, a few errant locks of white hair twirling in the breeze.

"That aroma, nothing like it...," says Endre, grinning all the while. "The scent of the faithful."

The albino lifts both of his arms silently upwards, his eyes closing as his head tilts back. It's some sort of unspoken signal. His brethren act on it immediately, descending on the men and women of the congregation like rabid dogs. Pastor Whitman thinks he must be hallucinating. Blood is spraying all around him, limbs actually becoming detached from bodies and tumbling to the asphalt. He sees the one that was hiding under the garbage bags slam into poor old Abigail, the man's teeth suddenly seeming like miniature knives in his gums, his eyes turning from mud-colored to gleaming yellow. Some of Abigail's blood speckles the priest's face as her throat is torn out. Pastor Whitman spins to the side, reaching out in vain, trying to help someone, anyone...just as those dark Twins seem to sprout sharpened bone-white claws from their fingertips and *shred* into three members of his flock, bits of clothing and flesh flying through the air. Some are attempting to flee, but the woman in black falls to all fours and leaps after them, tackling them to the ground, tearing into them with claws and teeth, giggling while she does it, her eyes like shining yellow lanterns set within her skull.

All around him, smeared carnage. The road decorated in trails of ruined meat, pieces of skin...parts of what used to be *people* only seconds ago. In the span in mere minutes, Pastor Whitman realizes that he is alone, his entire flock dead and dying, being torn at, being chewed upon, being *fed* upon.

The albino still stands before Pastor Whitman, making direct eye contact. The priest finds it very hard to meet that gaze in his shocked, horrified state. Those eyes look too much like the blood that surrounds him, the irises the very same shade of dark scarlet.

Pastor Whitman slowly backs up, the albino slowly stepping forward to match his pace. Muttered prayers leave the pastor's lips, his eyes fluttering up to the sky, seeming to search for something there, even the slightest glimmer of hope.

The pale one's voice cuts into him like a knife through butter, all gravelly and serrated.

"There's nothing worth seeing up there but Mother Moon, holy man. And beyond her? Deep, dark nothing. No salvation. No god to strike me down here in your hour of desperation..."

Pastor Whitman staggers back now, moving past the station wagon, his eyes trying to avoid the ravenous forms all around him that are tearing into corpses that were once his friends.

"Heavenly Father, hallowed be thy name," he mumbles, his fingers reaching up to touch his white collar for some kind of paltry comfort. "Please God; drive this pestilence from my sight."

The pale one throws back his head and laughs, ragged chuckles rising up from the barrel of his chest. Lizzie joins in, giggling wildly before pushing her face back down into the chest of a fallen body to nibble on a hunk of still expanding lung.

"You misguided cattle never fail to amuse me. You're begging for a god, holy man? You wanna see something miraculous?"

Endre Calder's mouth spreads open wider than humanly possible, those teeth shining and glimmering with saliva.

"Let me show you what a *god* really looks like..."

It starts with the sound of the albino's bones cracking within him, seeming to rearrange inside of his body. His muscles expand, splitting and rippling. His arms elongate, bone-colored claws bursting up from the fingernails. He becomes even larger (if that's possible) his frame twisting and contorting, spurts of saliva bursting out from teeth that are growing into huge, razor-tipped canines. The fur comes next, snow-white fur that pierces up through his skin and coats his entire body, becoming a thick, silky pelt. His shadow falls overtop Pastor Whitman, a low, menacing growl rising up from the dark corridor of his throat.

Pastor Whitman is barely cognizant of the fact that he has soiled himself. His eyes are wide, uncomprehending. The albino is no longer there. What stands in his place is a great white wolf...the monstrous beast so large and imposing that the priest resembles a child in comparison.

The priest doesn't even realize the full implications of what is happening to him when one of those enormous paws wraps around his throat, lifting him high into the air. Realization only comes when that second paw rams forward into his chest, the claws rending through his tissue and snapping back the ribs with relative ease. Only when the slavering white wolf has pulled his heart out of the aperture of his chest does Pastor Whitman realize his own doom, the atriums oozing, the torn ventricles splattered across the beast's open palm.

By the time Pastor Whitman is thrown to the asphalt with the open crater in his chest, all realizations are beyond him. Thoughts are beyond him. Breathing is beyond him. Even faith is beyond him as death closes black curtains over his eyes.

The white wolf casually tosses the priest's heart up into the air, letting it fly upwards before gravity brings it back down, and then he snaps it up into his jaws and swallows it like a mere appetizer.

That hideous transformation comes again, the bones cracking, the spine and limbs twisting and contorting, an ear-splitting howl roaring up past the lips of the albino as he returns to his human form. His lips and the bottom of his chin are absolutely saturated with Pastor Whitman's blood, and he lightly reaches up to wipe a hand across it, smacking his lips together a few times, seeming to appreciate the taste.

He turns momentarily to his brethren, watching them feed.

What he sees makes that grin return, fresh and rejuvenated.

Annihilation.

Total, complete annihilation.

"I thought the heart of a holy man might have a more appealing flavor than that. Seemed a tad tough and stringy. I'd give it 2 out of 5 stars on the pious gourmet scale."

More laughter from his brethren. Laughter amidst blood and annihilation.

***

For the entire length of this ambush, Grady has watched from the shadows beneath the birch tree. He's deeply unsettled, one of his hands twitching minutely at his side.

One of the congregation members is somehow clinging to life, crawling forward across the road and leaving a snail trail of grisly blood and meat behind him. One of The Twins sank claws into the unfortunate man's eye sockets, so he's crawling blind, his eyes just blackened holes dripping with eggshell white ooze. Endre slowly walks behind the crawling victim, making a motion towards Grady, calling the boy over to him.

Grady comes, albeit reluctantly, his breathing coming in and out of his mouth in short, clipped bursts.

"I know all of this is new to you, Grady...but sooner or later you're gonna have to actively participate. Let's start you off slow. Finish this one off," says Endre, one limb-sized arm slipping companionably across Grady's shoulders.

The boy remains motionless, his lips working, struggling to find words. He knows what's expected of him. He knows that in order to fit in, he must give himself over to this savagery, this primitive desire to maul and eviscerate. There's a part of him that *wants* to do it so badly. His eyes change for the briefest of moments, flashing with a yellow, animalistic glow, the pupils becoming tiny black pinpricks. But just as quickly, the yellow glow fades. His eyes return to their normal color.

A deeper part of him—the part that still has a conscience—whispers within his head, telling him that what is being done here is *wrong*. So horribly wrong…

"I don't think I'm ready just yet, Endre. I'm sorry…"

It comes out as little more than a mumble, Grady's eyes falling down to stare at his shoes. The albino sighs, his arm sliding away from Grady's shoulders. The boy thinks he's about to turn away, but with lightning quickness Endre grabs Grady by the head and *smashes* the side of his face up against one of the station wagon's windows, not hard enough to shatter the glass, but hard enough to send spiderweb cracks all the way through it.

Grady grits his teeth in pain, the pressure in his skull building as Endre presses his face harder and harder up against the glass.

"Sooner or later, you've gotta get with the fuckin' program, Grady. This is who we are. This is *what* we are. If you don't have the stomach or the balls for it, maybe you'd prefer to associate with the prey instead of the predators?" Endre snarls, finally stepping back and removing his hand from Grady's head. Grady gasps and falls to his hands and knees, one side of his face beet red from being wedged up against the glass. Raymond takes that moment to walk up and casually spit a wad of chewing tobacco right into Grady's hair before kicking the crawling victim with all of his force, the man's neck immediately snapping…his body becoming still.

The old man sniffs at the air, his gaze traveling farther down Meridian Drive in the direction of Main Street.

"I'm catching a whiff of somethin' down that way, Endre."

Endre shrugs, the rest of the members of the group already starting to gather up the corpses of the fallen.

"Maybe a straggler ran off. Go check it out…we'll get the rest of these meat-sacks back to the den."

Endre gestures down to Grady in mild disgust.

"And take the runt with you, Ray. My patience is wearing thin and I'm tired of looking at him for now. Try to school him in how to track, hunt, and actually *kill*."

"Can do," says Raymond, reaching down to roughly pull Grady up to his feet and push him in the direction of Main Street, both of them walking off together.

Lizzie and The Twins are already heading back towards the salvage yard, multiple corpses draped over their shoulders, carrying all that dead weight like it's absolutely nothing to them. A soft whimpering comes from the station wagon, Endre pausing for a moment to look into the driver's side window.

"Well, shit…I forgot all about you, Blake! Job well done. I promised you a bullet, didn't I?"

The sobs continue, Blake's chin resting against his chest.

Endre takes several steps back from the station wagon and removes his antique six shooter from his belt, taking a moment to aim the old pistol at Blake's head. He then smiles, moving his aim down the side of the station wagon until the barrel of the gun is pointed at the vehicle's gas tank.

He pulls the trigger, the slug slamming into the station wagon, a muffled explosion sending pluming flames into life all over the vehicle. Endre then starts walking off with the rest of his people, pausing only to stuff the six shooter back into his belt. Behind him, Blake's screams reach a crescendo as he's cooked alive, the station wagon now nothing more than an oven constructed of twisted metal.

The albino doesn't even bother to acknowledge Blake's immolation, his back turned as he keeps walking right on down the road.

15

Luther

I did not just see that. I did not just witness that. That was an impossible metamorphosis. I did not just watch that gargantuan man twist and contort his own bone structure to turn into an equally gargantuan animal. A big, bad *wolf*.

It had to be a hallucination. It had to be just a surreal daydream. I spent much of last night tossing and turning, sleepless and stressed...so that must be the answer. I simply dozed off behind this fence and dreamt of savagery and unspeakable transformations. But why then do the others look as shocked as I do? Why is Mallory's face so ashen and pale? Where are Vic's eyes as wide as saucers? Why even is Asher—usually unshakable in his resolve—staring out from these broken boards like a man who just saw something that is totally beyond the realm of everyday reality?

I don't have time to continue with these internal musings. Two are them are heading in this direction, that station wagon nothing but a burning metal effigy left in the middle of the road. It's that filthy, limping fiend with the unkempt beard and a boy who looks no older than eighteen or nineteen. They're coming towards the fence, both of them seeming to pause at certain intervals to sniff the air. They inhale the air currents...like hounds seeking a quarry.

Asher is pulling at my sleeve. He's pulling and whispering at all of us. He's telling us we *must* get away from here. We must run back to the safety of the vault before they find our flimsy hiding spot. We are moving now, but I'm only dimly aware of it. Those visuals are still in my brain, corrosive sights, a spill of acid in my thoughts. Humans torn to bloody ribbons. That thumping heart—the heart of a priest—devoured like a delectable hors d'oeuvre. And that hideous, lingering howl. I hear it still in my ears, haunting me, bedeviling me...even as I stumble down the narrow space between two houses, following along behind Asher and the rest.

Those two behind us are fast. That old man should be slow—he has the look of a grizzled, beaten soul—but his gait is far too speedy. The boy comes along with him. I don't think they've spotted us yet, but they're so close. We try to dart around a corner, but we're lead to a dead end with a thick chain link fence blocking our passage. There are only two options. The back door to the general store, the lock already broken and the door hanging halfway open, and the melted remnants of a milk truck to the right. It might be possible to make it through the back of the milk truck and out the open passenger's side door; a shortcut back to Cobalt Street, but time is running so terribly short.

The footsteps behind us are too close, stomping and intent. It's a moment of uncertainty, chaos bleeding into all decision making. I make for the entry into the general store, pulling Mallory along with me. She immediately pushes Cara towards Asher and Vic, motioning towards the slumped milk truck, whispering for them to get her back to the vault by any means necessary. There's no time left. There are no options left. Our little group must fracture...or face immediate ruin.

Asher locks eyes with Mallory, something passing between them, and then he snatches up Cara and runs for the milk truck, Vic trailing behind them and trying to look everywhere at once. Mallory and I duck behind the broken door of the general store with just seconds to spare.

We almost catch a glimpse of the treacherous twosome pursuing us just as we all split apart. I think we all avoided their eyes by just a millisecond or so. I hope in the most optimistic part of myself that we did...

Now in these grave moments of panic, it is only our scents that may serve to betray us...

***

I've got my hand locked around Mallory's forearm, leading her down aisles that have been totally ransacked. Cartons of milk have been smashed across the floor, entire shelves swept by violent hands, objects broken and scattered all across the tiles. I knew based on the broken lock that the fiends had already been through here on that first fateful night in town, but there must be some temporary hiding place for us. Some reprieve from the hounds on our heels...

We run past the frozen food coolers, the glass shattered, the bottles inside either clawed or smashed or shot to pieces with bludgeoning bullets. A mildly rotten odor assaults my nostrils, and I see the source of it as we near the front of the store. The owner is laid out across the counter, one leg propped up forever on the cash register. His entire torso is a mutilated mess, the corpse sporting wounds inflicted by only the sharpest of teeth and claws. To add insult to injury, the fiends stuffed a can of beets into the dead man's mouth, the can protruding there from his shredded lips. The corpse has started to attract flies, a few lazy, fat green ones buzzing greedily nearby. I pull Mallory in a new direction just as the door we entered from smashes open. No time left. We hide or we die.

Both of us dive down behind the counter, my satchel of books falling from my shoulder, the precious hardbacks falling out across the floor. We crouch there, the flies buzzing atop our heads, fear eating through our hearts...our eyes locking and sharing an unspoken message.

Both Mallory and I seem to have the same idea as we hear the footsteps tramping through the general store.

She motions to her mouth and nose, and then immediately nods towards me. I nod back. We must attempt to hold our breath.

We can't risk these men hearing even a few inhalations or exhalations leaving our nostrils or our lips...

16

Grady

I can still feel the slimy ooze of Raymond's chewing tobacco dripping down the back of my neck. The humiliation is even worse, to have faltered there in front of Endre and the rest of the pack. Maybe there's just something different about me, but I can't take to cold-blooded murder like the rest of them do. To them it seems like nothing at all, just an instinctual extinguishing of lives...but the guilt of something like that is too much for me to bear. I've already done things in service to this pack that absolutely haunt me, things that I'll never be able to redeem myself for. But kill for them? Tear open human beings like they're nothing but sacks of blood and shit? That's not who I am. That's not the person I am even with the animalistic impulses that sometimes light sparks in my head.

When we came into the alley, Ray's eyes were on the open door of the general store, but I looked through the back of the milk truck. I caught the briefest glimpse of two men running off down the road and carrying a little girl, the sight of them obscured by the shattered windshield. I said nothing of this to Raymond. I wanted them to get away. I want those people to survive this...

Raymond is clomping through the general store now, sniffing at the air, his mud-encrusted boots kicking various cans and boxes out of his way.

"If you gonna hunt with me, little shit...you gonna do it the right way. You hear me?"

I grunt in response, keeping pace with the sour old man as he sweeps his eyes from aisle to aisle.

"Lots of smells in here. Curdled milk. Rotten eggs. Booze dripping outta shattered bottles. But beneath those smells? What we lookin' for. You gotta learn to isolate the scents..."

Raymond reaches one of the large beer coolers, proceeding to reach forward and haul it back with all his strength, the cooler crashing down to the floor. There's no one hiding behind it. He snarls in frustration, still searching.

"They in here. I know they in here. I smell strawberry shampoo on a head of womanly hair. I smell sweat dripping outta living pores. I even smell that bitter cream that old men rub into their hands to soothe arthritis..." Raymond grins, his brown tombstone teeth stained forever by his tobacco addiction.

Raymond reaches forward and pushes me towards the front of the store, my body stumbling to the side as a few jars of pickles roll off a shelf and clatter to the floor. This cantankerous old wretch...words barely describe how much I detest him.

"You gotta learn, Grady. Endre getting real tired of your cowardly shit. If you run with us, you better be willing to get them hands dirty and bloody. It ain't a pretty world out there for one of our kind all by his or her lonesome," says Raymond, his gnarled hand reaching forward to push a magazine rack out of his way. "A lonewolf gonna end up a dead wolf sooner or later."

We both stop for a moment near the counter, noticing the body that's still lying there and swarming with flies.

"Remind me we gotta collect that one too. Best get him back to the den before the flies get the sweet parts."

"Maybe you just smelled him, Ray? I didn't see any stragglers leave the chapel. How about we just load him up and get back before Endre starts wondering where we are?"

I hope the question will dissuade Raymond, but instead he just pivots on his heels and sends an open slap right into my cheek, the sting of it lingering, the sound like a small firearm going off in the confines of the general store. My lips tighten, anger building inside of me, but still I do nothing. I'm supposed to "know" my place...

"My nose don't lie, little shit. There ain't just decaying meat in here. There's *fresh* meat too. And there it be again, that smell that just gives me the shivers...that strawberry shampoo."

Raymond's eyes drift to the counter and whatever might lie beyond the counter. He starts heading around the wooden barrier, his nostrils flaring wider and wider, that feral, familiar gleam starting to show in his gaze. I know that look well. It's a look that promises dirty, nasty things to come.

Suddenly we both dart around the counter...and there they are. Two unfortunate souls, a woman and an elderly man. If only they had gotten away in time. If only they had managed to avoid this...

They're both already rising up to their feet, the fear baking off of them in waves, the aroma of it almost choking me.

Raymond's tongue slips out to lick crackly, dried out lips. Something like white ooze appears in the corners of his mouth, a foaming dog, a dog in heat...

His wormy gaze crawls over the woman, tracing the curves of her body, slobber starting to actually drip down his chin now.

"Well fuck me sideways, ain't you got a lil' body on you, strawberry pie? You smell...just like a big ol' field full of strawberries. Do you feel like em' too? All soft and squishy?"

The woman reaches down desperately, picking up a hardback book as a poor excuse for a weapon. Ray just chuckles. The old man standing beside her is taking up a defensive stance too, his weak, withered hands held up into balled fists.

"I'm gonna find out...and this grandpappy you with ain't gonna stop me. I wanna taste me some strawberries..."

The tension holds for a moment or two longer, an infinitesimal standoff.

And then Raymond pounces...

***

It all happens incredibly fast. The blonde woman smashes the book into the side of Raymond's face with all her might, and as expected, it has no effect at all. He pushes her squarely in the chest, sending her sprawling down behind the counter. The old man lunges toward Raymond and attempts to grapple with him, but Ray easily overpowers the old-timer and tosses him over the counter and directly into a shelf full of cereal boxes. The old man crumples down in a heap, momentarily unconscious.

Raymond turns back to the woman on the floor, watching with intense pleasure as she crab walks backwards, scrabbling in a desperate attempt to put distance between herself and her attacker even though there's nowhere for her to go. Raymond has already torn the piece of straw that serves as his belt from his crusty trousers, and now he's slowly unzipping his fly. He laps at his lips, the slobber dripping down to hit the floor, droplet after droplet, a little foamy puddle starting to form there.

"I figure I'll fuck ya before I kill ya. And then after I've killed ya and gutted ya? I'll fuck ya again. Warm body or cold body...don't make no difference to me."

Raymond allows his body to fall down on top of the woman, his dirty hands digging at her clothing, ripping and tearing at her blouse. He turns back to me for a moment, that leering, grimy grin wider than ever on his bearded mug.

"Just gonna stand and watch, little shit? Bout time you participate. Bout time you get a piece. I'll let you take a turn on her lil' pink bunghole after I finish. Gotta turn a *boy* into a man of action..."

I'm watching Raymond tear this woman's clothes to shreds, the tears forming in her eyes, her golden hair all wild and tangled around her face. I'm hearing his slimy words drift into my eardrums. I realize that I'm at a crossroads in my life right now. I have a choice. Stand here and let Raymond rape and mutilate this woman...or do something entirely unexpected. Something that would immediately make me an outcast among my own kind. The moral dilemma passes through my thoughts for only a brief second or two before I decide just which road I want to take...

"You're right, Ray. It's time for me to participate. It's time for me...to be a man of action."

It's growing in me, that animal inside, purging up through the forearms and the gums in my mouth. The bone claws split out from beneath my fingernails, becoming like natural butcher knives. My teeth grow in my mouth, little pains infecting the gum line, but I'm used to it. It doesn't take long for the canines to elongate, for my mouth to become the mouth of a great white shark.

Raymond turns his attention back to me just as my eyes take on that deep yellow glow, and then I'm on him, thrashing my claws down across the stained flannel of his shirt, shredding into the flesh of his back, tearing so violently that pieces of skin and cloth go flying from side to side. Raymond growls in pain, his hands immediately reaching towards his injured back.

My hand comes down for another slash, but the old man catches my forearm and rises up to his feet, and when he headbutts me with all of his force, I realize just how much stronger he is compared to me. His forehead smashes into my own like a small boulder and I'm knocked down into a display filled with cigarettes, my eyes glazed, my entire body seeming momentarily numb. I'm dazed...dangerously close to just blacking out.

"You turn on your *OWN*, boy? You sink claws into your own kin? You're finished now. You're fuckin' fate is death between Endre's jaws...but not before I put a whole heap of hurt onto you."

Ray moves towards me, lifting up a boot to smash it down into my face, but the woman reaches out and grabs hold of his ankle. He turns back to her, a frustrated growl forming in the back of his throat. He falls back down on her just as she reaches desperately for more weapons, picking up multiple hardback books and just slamming them into his head over and over again. They bounce off like nothing, totally ineffective. Moby Dick goes flying. The Picture of Dorian Gray bounces from cheek to the floor. She rams Great Expectations into Ray's chin, and he simply swats it out her hands like a bothersome mosquito. His eyes begin to glow now, lanterns in his dirt-stained sockets, and the teeth are slowly growing, slowly sharpening. I just make it out through hazy eyes as the woman reaches for a final book, some big clunky thing that looks to be bound with hard metallic surfaces.

The woman seizes this book in one hand and *whips* it into the side of Raymond's temple as hard as she possibly can. This time the reaction is totally different. Raymond actually *screams*, an acrid burning smell rising up from the flesh of his face. He rolls off the woman, reaching towards his temple, and his hand draws back with bits of melted skin and blood grimed across his fingertips.

The woman seems to make some internal realization. She wastes no time at all, seizing on the opportunistic moment to preserve her own survival. She grabs hold of that same book, and as I squint past the blurry mound of cigarette boxes that have fallen across my chest, I see what that book is bound in.

Silver. Pure, lustrous silver.

The woman takes the book up in both hands and brings it down on top of Raymond's head as hard as she possibly can. He tries to throw his forearms up and block it, but it's no use, the book connects again, smashing down against his pate and sending little tendrils of smoke up from his burning, blackening hair. I've never seen Raymond helpless before. I've never seen Raymond in a position like this, that low, treacherous cunning seeming to always pull him out of bleak situations…

Not this time. The woman keeps on smashing the book down onto his head, a primitive roar seeming to rise out of her lips each time she does it. Raymond is being battered and smashed, his head starting to cave in, little gray tendrils of brain-matter oozing out of his ears. The silver-bound book falls and falls until nothing is left of Raymond's face but blood, brains, and ruin.

Raymond is no more. That silver corrodes his flesh, lingering there and sending up such an awful smell.

At the hands of this brave, mortal woman, the pack just lost a member…

17

Mallory

I keep pulling at my hair, pulling and pulling, trying to get the gristle out. I realize that I need to stop doing this, but it feels like a compulsion, something I can't stop doing. I guess I'm in a state of shock. I don't stop until Luther finally stumbles over to me, a darkening bruise on the side of his head. He stands protectively over me, glaring at the boy that remains.

"I just killed a man..."

The words slip out of my mouth, breathless, powerless. I'm trembling next to a body that I just battered into lifelessness. I don't know what happened. It was just fight or flight...and fight kicked into overdrive. The boy hears me despite how quiet my whisper was, even stepping forward to respond.

"Not a man, ma'am. He stopped being a man a long time ago..."

Luther crowds closer to me, his lips pulled down tightly as he stares daggers into the young man.

"Stay away. Don't come any close," says Luther, his old, gnarled fingers trying to help me wipe some of the blood from my tangled hair.

I finally find my voice, and with it I find my strength, actually grabbing the side of the counter to haul myself up to a vertical base. My feet feel a bit wobbly, but I think they'll support me.

"No, Luther. He...tried to save me."

I stare at the boy, taking in his dirty blonde hair, his almost naïve features. He can't be even twenty years old yet...

"I should go," says the boy, turning uncertain eyes towards the exit door. Before I even realize what I'm doing, my hand reaches out to catch his shoulder, stopping him.

"I heard this piece of vermin say your name while we were hiding. Grady, right?" I'm Mallory...and this is Luther."

My eyes lock on the boy's eyes, the contact lingering. He can barely hold the gaze for long, his eyes averting almost shyly.

"I don't know what you are...but I know you're nothing like him," I gesture to the rotten creature I was just forced to dispatch. "Thank you for what you did. Thank you for trying to stop it."

I never could have predicted his reaction. The tears that well up in his eyes, spilling down his cheeks silently. He reminds me of a kid fresh out of high school. Young. Misguided. So terribly confused...

"I didn't want this. I didn't want to be....*this*."

He shows me his hand for a moment, those strange, calcified bone claws extending for just a moment before he retracts them back into his fingertips. Luther's voice is behind me, sounding worried and nervous.

"We need to go, Mallory. We have to get back to the others..."

I decide to take a chance. Based on what this boy has done, he's bought my trust, hook, line, and sinker. Will I regret this decision? Maybe. I don't think I will. It's something in his eyes. A lost, broken sorrow.

"Come back with us, Grady. We have a safe place. We can figure this out."

"Mallory, that isn't a good idea," warns Luther, that same tinge of deep concern coating his words. I wave him off.

"You said it yourself. You're not like the rest of *them*. What you just tried to do for me? It makes you so much *better* than the rest of them. So much more human."

This time he doesn't look away when I catch his eyes. His jaw is set, his eyes watery pools that trickle beneath the store's flickering fluorescents.

"Come back with us..."

He turns to look at the door again, almost like he's seconds away from just running back out of it. He seems to find something inside of him, and he finally looks back at me, offering but a single word. "Okay."

18

Asher

Cara sits in one corner of the vault, surrounded by children's books, her tiny hands fluttering across her sleeves and picking at them nervously. She's been asking "where's mommy?" over and over again. I wish I had an answer for her.

Vic sits at the table, his head in his hands, obviously in a state of total disbelief due to the events we witnessed outside of that chapel. I understand his confusion. I'm feeling the exact same thing, this needling, festering thought in my head—almost like a parasite dining on my brain—what in the hell were those *things* that tore those people apart like they were nothing but thin broomsticks of bone covered in sacks of easily punctured blood?

I'm pacing from side to side near the circular door, my hands on my hips. It's been too long. There's been absolutely no sign of Mallory or Luther. Why did we split up in the first place? It all seemed to happen in a few brief blinks, just milliseconds of time with such heavy implications weighing on those moments. The group fractured, torn cleanly in two—almost like the bodies of those poor souls that were lured out of the doors of their sanctuary on Meridian Drive.

"I'm going back out, Vic. You've gotta stay with Cara. They've been out there too long...I have to find them..."

Cara's eyes turn to big, wide saucers, and Vic finally raises his head and then his heavy frame up from the chair, shaking his head fiercely from side to side. The man looks both terrified and bewildered, a strange mixture of facial expressions twisting at his ruddy features.

"You cannot go out there, Asher. None of us can even think about opening that fuckin' door. You saw what I saw, didn't you? I don't...I don't understand it. None of it makes any goddamned sense!"

Vic's voice rises with panic, the tone almost unbecoming of such a cocksure man, nothing like the Vic I met when Luther first ushered us into this safe haven.

"I don't understand it either, Vic. I don't have even the vaguest idea, but I know we can't leave Mallory and Luther out there with those things. We saw what they are. We *know* what they can do now..."

Vic lightly takes hold of my shirt, motioning me closer to a darkened corner of the library's inner sanctum. He even lowers his voice for Cara's benefit, nothing but a brittle whisper emerging from his mouth.

"They're not people, Asher. There ain't a damn bit of rationality connected to any of it. They murdered those people...and they were *eating* parts of them right there in the middle of the street."

Vic swipes a hand across his mouth, his lips suddenly wet with too much saliva. His eyes are all twitching nerves, swirling doubt.

"I ain't the sort of man to admit when I'm wrong, but I'll do it now. You cannot go out that door. You cannot take a single step beyond this library. They're *monsters*, Asher. There's no other word for it. There's no other word for what those things did and for what those things became..."

He pauses, his hands still plastered across my shirt, both of the palms wet with sweat, his brow practically dripping with it.

"Monsters. Hungry, hellborn monsters."

I'm about to respond, but something cuts our conversation off and leaves both of us standing there in ominous, unspoken horror.

Three loud knocks at the vault door.

Rap. Rap. Rap.

The rapping and the tapping and the knocking of something that desperately wants to be let inside.

19

Mallory

I can hear loud voices behind the door, Luther and Grady standing behind me, both of them looking uncertain about how this is going to go. I knock once more, this time yelling out "it's Mallory!" and the argument beyond the vault door ceases. Seconds later the door swings open, and standing there is Asher, those slate-gray eyes looking so thankful to see us all intact.

I rush straight for Cara, my little girl hopping up from her corner to wrap her arms round my leg, nuzzling at me like a kitten would. Luther steps into the vault, and behind him Grady reluctantly follows. Vic steps forward to welcome Luther back, but as soon as he sees Grady, his eyes practically bug right out of his head. His hand scrabbles across the table for his crowbar, and he immediately seizes upon it and blunders forward towards Grady.

"ONE OF THEM GOT INSIDE!"

Vic is already reaching his arm back to swing that weapon at Grady's head, the young man's eyes taking on that shimmering yellow shade that can only mean bad things to come. I'm able to race across the room just in time, placing my own body in front of Grady and stopping Vic with the crowbar still raised up high above his head.

"No, Vic. You don't understand..."

"I understand just fine, Mallory. Move aside...this is one of those *animals.* We let him in here and we're all mincemeat before the night is through."

Asher is moving forward now, silently doing what he can to try and help me keep this situation under control. He's placed his own body between Vic and Grady as well, one hand reaching up to lightly pull Vic's forearm down. That crowbar slowly lowers...but Vic's limbs look like snakes just waiting to snap outward again at even a moment's notice.

"This animal saved my life, Vic," I admit, Luther even confirming it with a brief nod in the background. "One of the meanest and nastiest of them hunted Luther and I down and tried to murder us. None of us would be alive right now if not for Grady."

I turn back to the boy, his eyes once again sheepishly falling to the floor. Asher moves forward, seeming to try his best to get down to the gritty truth of all this. I trust in his ability to do so. I'm so tired, my only desire right now to curl up in the corner and hug my daughter tighter that I've ever hugged her in my entire life.

Asher takes a moment to study Grady, looking the boy up and down.

"If what Mallory says is true—and I have no reason to doubt her—we all owe you a debt of gratitude. Thank you."

Asher actually extends his hand to the boy, Grady staring down it for a long time, almost like he's forgotten what he's supposed to do. That's how long he's been separated from the human part of himself. Even shaking hands has become a foreign concept...

After a long, drawn out moment...Grady clasps that hand and shakes with Asher. Something passes between them. Mutual respect. I get the feeling that Grady understands that if anyone would really listen to him, it's Asher. It's that kind, inquisitive look in Asher's eyes. That look can disarm just about anyone...

"You have the look of a man who has a tale to tell, Grady."

Asher works to close up the vault door, Vic looking on sullenly but maintaining his silence for the moment. Asher then motions to the table in the center of the library's inner sanctum.

"Please sit. Help us to understand...all of this," says Asher.

Grady sighs, running a hand along the peach fuzz on his cheek. He sits. He looks at all of us, his mouth opening prematurely and then closing again.

"It's hard to know where to even start..."

20

Grady's Tale

It happened exactly two years ago. I was hiking in Blanchard State Forest, one of Washington's most picturesque stretches of wilderness. I've always been an avid hiker; I'd call it one of my biggest hobbies...so I was fully prepared for even the most challenging trails that I might encounter out there.

What I wasn't prepared for was the animal attack just as darkness started to fall, the full, bright moon rising up to dominate the sky above the treetops. The animal looked sickened, weak and extremely frail. It was dark and I barely saw anything, just some lumbering, blackened beast with mangy fur that flashed out from behind a boulder and sank dirty claws into the left side of my chest, right across the pectoral muscle. The animal never stopped moving after that, it seemed to just topple down a ridge on the other side of the trail and then limp off into the heavy foliage beyond.

The wound wasn't too terribly deep, the lacerations were actually pretty shallow, so I was able to disinfect them and patch them up with the first aide kit that I always carry along with me during my hikes. My chief concern was rabies...so I planned to consult with the park rangers and then promptly see a physician after I came down from the trail head. I just assumed it was a confused black bear stumbling out of hibernation, just lashing out for the pure sake of being surprised at the pink, two-legged creature that stood before it.

I was wrong. I was so very wrong...

Those park rangers never found a bear in that area. They never found anything at all. The doctor I saw gave me some antibiotics to prevent infection, but he said the wound looked clean and there was no sign of the rabies virus in any of the saliva samples or skin biopsies that they took from me. He sent me along with prescription in hand, and I figured that would be the end of it. Just a freak accident during a hike. I thought it would be good story tell my friends back in Seattle sometime...

I went back to work just like usual. I was a barista in a coffee shop, nothing special, but it paid the rent on my little studio apartment. I didn't know about the lunar phases then. I didn't know why I was starting to feel agitated, easily angered...even lashing out at coworkers occasionally. It wasn't me. I've always been a pretty mellow guy. There was this feeling that's hard to describe. It's like moths fluttering beneath your skin, smacking their soft bodies inside of your flesh, desperate to come out, desperate to be unleashed...

It got so much worse during the half moon. I didn't connect anything to the moon then; I was just some ignorant kid from Seattle peddling fancy coffee and treading trails in my free time. I didn't understand the hunger burning in my guts. I couldn't comprehend why my bones seemed to occasionally twist and realign themselves at momentary intervals, my knuckles constantly cracking all on their own.

One day I just walked out the front door of the coffee shop I worked at and never returned. I did it because the smells had started to overwhelm me. It seems I never noticed them before, but it became a full assault on my nostrils. Earthy coffee grounds. Thick, pulsating creamer. The stench of the very foam cups which I poured the coffee into...

And worst of all? The people in the shop. Their sweat. Their body odor. The lightest layer of dirt grimed across their pores. Women with nauseating perfume and men with gel in their hair that smelled like grape jelly left out in the sun for too long. It just about drove me batshit crazy.

There was an undersmell, though. A scent beneath all those impure chemicals and creams and ointments and everything else people slather themselves with these days. The smell of living, breathing flesh. Blood running through veins, traveling through ventricles, pumping into so many meaty hearts. I started to like that smell. It became mildly intoxicating, like a good buzz when you're on the way to getting black out drunk. I started to worry about how much I liked it...

***

I knew she was coming. I knew soon she'd rise to make the stars seem like dwarves in comparison, all that brightness, all that fullness. It felt like an actual calendar flipping through my thoughts, her final phase just hours away.

My bones sang wretched, mournful songs to me. My heart hammered so hard I feared it might burst through the flesh of my chest. I knew something was inside of me. Something was buried there in a very shallow grave, clothed only in the barest layer of human skin...something digging and clawing and gnawing to be free. I'll never forget that first turn. I learned later from Endre that the first turn kills off the great majority of our kind. Some simply don't have the willpower to endure the transformation. It takes great mental fortitude to survive the transition, the reshaping of your own physical body, the skeletal parts moving and slithering inside of you like hardened, betraying eels. Some have instant brain aneurisms. Others have fatal heart attacks. A few perish from the sheer shock of that initial turn. That's why our species is nearly extinct, a mere handful of us alive and breathing on every continent of this planet.

Beneath the pale light of that full, bloated moon...it overtook me. I can never describe to you what it feels like. The pain was unbearable that first time—it lessens with each turn that comes after—but it never really goes away. My flesh sprouting splinters of fur, my fingertips splitting into jagged claws, my skull cracking and elongating to form a muzzle filled with row after row of serrated teeth.

You never forget your first. I never forgot mine...

I was lucky. I'd managed to slink off into a heavily wooded area when I felt the alien sensations inside of me becoming worse by the minute. I was afforded the luxury of turning in isolation, my only witnesses the crickets hiding in the underbrush and the bats circling the treetops. After the pain finally abated, I was left with one of the most peculiar feelings imaginable. It's nothing like the old legends claim. It can't be compared to something you see on a television show or in a Hollywood movie. You don't become this mindless, rabid beast that remembers nothing of the turn when you transition back to your human form after Mother Moon wanes.

The best way to explain it? The perfect blending of human and wolf. It's a form of symbiosis. 50% of your mind retains rationality, the ability to control your actions, to think and strategize...all basic human brain functions. The other 50% is pure instinctual bloodlust. That's the wolf-mind...the part of you that longs to run, to drink in the night scents, to hunt and kill and bury your teeth in shredded meat.

It's pure power...so addictive, so seductive. You feel invulnerable. You feel like a massive, heavily muscled titan that can stand against absolutely anything that is thrown at you. I came upon a doe that night, just drinking from a little babbling brook, none the wiser to the glowing eyes watching her from the cover of brambly thorns.

She never had a chance. I wrenched her head cleanly from her neck and drank down the sweet nectar of her life's blood, and then I spent what remained of the night with my face buried in the red crater of her belly, just dining, having my fill...

You retain all of those thoughts. You remember everything. I remember how I felt that night. The wolf-mind wanted me to open up the deer and taste the warm flesh...and the human-mind seemed to think it acceptable as well. Better than hunting down another person and tearing that poor soul apart. So we comprised...me and the wolf within.

That's one of the biggest aspects of living as a lycanthrope. You must learn to compromise. The wolf-mind and the human-mind must settle together on a firm choice, and together they act on that choice. That night the compromise was the death of a doe. In the grand scheme of things? Not so terrible. Not so ungodly.

Even so, when I woke the next day to the cold dawn with that equally cold deer corpse beside me and my mouth and upper torso awash in dried plasma, I knew that my old life had ended permanently. I remembered the ripping, the tearing, and that impulse to throw back my head and howl long and hard for Mother Moon...

I had no idea what I was then. I didn't know what I had become or how it was even possible in any realistic sense. All I knew was that I had become something new and extremely dangerous, something MORE than human...and something capable of extreme destruction. I knew Mother Moon would bring it out in me again the next time she unfurled her dark robes and showed me her fullest self. At the moment when you receive that bite or that swipe of claws from another lycanthrope and you live through it, your connection to Mother Moon begins. It's like an umbilical cord in your head, reaching down from that cratered surface high in the sky and filling you up with instincts and desires and the overwhelming need to embrace the animal side.

The old me died during that hike through the forest...

And the new me realized that I needed to get far away from a largely populated city like Seattle before the next turn...

***

I used what little money I had saved up to travel to one of the most remote regions I could think of. The wilds of Alaska...specifically a little town on the edge of the Bering Sea called Nome. There was a bit of a gold rush happening there, but the other major trade that almost any man could find work in was the fishing business. I found dirty, thankless work very quickly after arriving...just gutting and cleaning fish on one of the docks. I kept to myself and spent the endless days sinking that serrated blade into white fish bellies and spilling the contents out across the damp boards of the dock. Other men worked alongside me, but we rarely spoke to each other. It seemed the cold and the nature of our work simply sapped all desire to be jovial or start any sort of conversation. I'll never forget those bearded, hollow-eyed faces that loomed beside me as the setting sun turned the Bearing Sea to frigid fire, their hands pruned and stained with salmon innards, just the same as my own hands. Those men had their demons too, I'm sure. They kept their demons close to the chest and never spoke of them, same as me. The only difference is that my demon actually lived inside of my chest, always breathing, always snarling in the far back of my mind, and patiently waiting for the freedom it so desperately desired.

Nome was a small enough town and I knew I could get out into the barren country before the next full moon rose, but something impeded my progress on the night before. I was leaving one of the many little dive bars in town, my mind fuzzy with drink and my hands still stinking from the day's work.

They came upon me on a barren stretch of beach, far beyond even the squatter's shacks that were out that way. I don't know how or why I went down that far, I just felt like walking. There were three of them. I remember how they moved, so quick, darting together as one, flashing in and out of my line of vision. Somehow deep down in my heart, I realized these three men knew what I was. They knew about the secret I was harboring. It seems silly to call them men now knowing what they really are. Their kind has words for us. Rabid dogs. Stinking hounds. Mangy moon-shifters. Endre has words for their species too. Mosquitoes. Classy corpses. Dead lampreys. It all comes down to just racial slurs in the end. When I was originally attacked on the hike, I could barely wrap my head around the fact that what I was becoming was actually a real thing. The simple fact that werewolves—that word was bound to be used sooner or later, so best to get it out now—were more than just fiction and myth. The same is true for their counterpart. Vampires exist. I know very little about them, only what I've been told and Endre is the only one who does the telling. He says they tend to live in great coven houses, families numbering in the twenties and thirties sometimes. He says they never die because they're dead already, sustained only by the animating blood of those that still live. He says they look down upon us and we look down upon them. He says occasionally they travel in small roving bands of two or three, but these are rare, usually just scouts for coven houses in the area.

I guess those three followed me because on some level they just sensed what I was. I realized quickly what they were too—I could smell it. The lack of warm, tantalizing meat. Their bodies just cold and empty sacks sloshing with plasma that immediately goes cold the moment it passes down their throats.

They descended upon me silently, no words, no exchange of pleasantries. They smashed and kicked at me like a weed in a garden, something that offended them and must be destroyed simply for the sake of destruction. I fought them hard, held my own for a moment or two, but they were so damn fast...

Soon they had me curled into the fetal position, my cheek pressed against cold, wet sand, those kicks preternaturally strong, boots ramming into my ribs over and over again.

I figured it was over. A part of me thought it a fitting end. How could I ever live an ordinary life with this slavering thing inside of me, all teeth and claws, as much a part of me now as the hair on my head or the skin on my bones?

Maybe those mosquitoes were doing me a favor. Maybe it was a mercy. I'll never know, because that was the first time I saw Endre. He was standing there on top of a dune, wearing tattered jeans and a black tank top. I wondered why he wasn't cold up there in that attire—but I realized later that it was because he was just like me, and our blood tends to run hot.

He was so pale, his wild white hair being torn at by the breeze coming in from the sea. The kicks were forcing me to roll across the sand now, my bloodied face being kissed by the lap of tidal waves. One of my eyes was puffed closed by that time, so I barely saw him walking down from the top of that dune. I barely saw him pulling that tank top up off his scarred torso. I noticed quickly that the kicks had stopped. I tried to look up at the mosquitoes, and it became apparent that something had changed in them. Moments ago they were confident and vicious in their efforts to kick me to pieces. Now they muttered to one another in some thick, old tongue...and I could have sworn I heard one of them whisper..."we should run."

They never got the chance to run. I suppose they fought him, but it all comes back to me in a red haze. I just remember glimpses of a massive white wolf tearing into strangely bloodless bodies. I remember limbs and bits of meat and pieces of cold flesh flying all around me. I was trying to push myself up to my side, coughing raggedly, and a severed bald head fell down inches from my face. Just the slightest trickle of blood oozed from the shredded stump of the throat, blood almost black in the night, oozing and thick like frozen molasses.

I flipped myself onto my back just as I heard his bones cracking and rearranging. I stared up at the stars above the Bering Sea and Endre stepped into my line of vision, towering there like some ivory-carved monolith. His mouth and chest were saturated in that blackish blood, but still he smiled at me, showing me teeth with bits of cold meat still grimed across the enamel.

He reached a pale hand down towards me...and he spoke to me for the very first time. I'll always remember what he said.

"It's been so long since I've found another..."

***

Everything I know about what I am, I've learned from Endre and the others. Lizzie is a fairly unreliable narrator about past events because she's a madwoman, Endre literally plucked her out of an asylum sometime during the Victorian era with the sole purpose of turning her because he thought she had beautiful, sea-blue eyes. She told me it was the night before she was scheduled to have a frontal lobotomy when he peeled the bars open on her cell window and whisked her away into a new lycanthropic life. My personal theory is that the eyes aren't the only reason Endre turned her. Endre is morbidly curious...has been ever since I've known him. It's my belief that he turned a woman who was already a certifiable lunatic simply to see what would happen. A horrible truth, but a truth nonetheless. She's the oldest aside from Endre.

The Twins are easier to communicate with and I always go to them if Endre isn't around. The Twins are Sudanese mutes, but they're accomplished writers and have answered almost every question I've asked of them. Endre turned them sometime in the 70s when a famine was sweeping their country. He found them lying frail and starving in the barren plains near a dry creek bed. They'd been tracking a wounded antelope out of sheer hunger and desperation. They'd finally felled the animal with a spear near the creek bed, but both brothers collapsed from exhaustion before they could even field dress the carcass. Endre was traveling in Africa in those days and he came across the brothers in their final moments. He admired their tenacity and their survival instinct. He saw parts of himself in The Twins, born hunters to their very core. It was that admiration that earned both Jok and Thon the bite that saved and extended their lives...

Raymond—the one Mallory killed—is almost not even worth a mention. Raymond was turned in the Appalachians just about six years ago. He didn't even notice the claw marks until he woke up from his drunken haze next to his moonshine still. I assume he was a sour old man in his human life, and the turn only soured him more. Endre just wanted a stupid, loyal dog in the form of Raymond, someone to round out the ranks of the pack and do most of the dirty work. Raymond filled that role perfectly.

Endre introduced me to the whole pack after we'd traveled to Canada. They'd been camped up in the Yukon for almost a full year, a place that sticks out in my mind as one of the most beautiful landscapes on this entire planet. Mountain ranges across every horizon, endless seas of evergreen trees, and rivers so crystal clear you could see every detail of your own face mirrored in the water. Endre was quick to get me there and out of Alaska. He told me the reason I'd been attacked was because a new coven house had recently been erected in Anchorage and it wasn't safe for any of our kind to stick around an area harboring too many mosquitoes.

I was happy to follow his lead. He knew things and he was quick to impart that knowledge to me. His charisma was like a vacuum; you just felt the pull of it and could hardly resist being drawn in. He taught me about partial turns—the ability to obtain a deep level of concentration through meditation and bring forth the claws and teeth even when Mother Moon is not full in the sky. All lycanthropes that have been turned can only fully transform during the brightest night of the lunar phase—the full moon—but partials turns can be performed whenever necessary to defend against foes or to aide in hunting, etc.

I found out Endre is what's called a "pureborn"...which essentially means that he was birthed into this world with the lupine gene already etched into his DNA. He was never bitten. He was never turned. He's been a lycanthrope since the moment he opened his eyes as an infant. Pureborns are extremely powerful entities, universally feared by other lycanthropes and mosquitoes alike. They're capable of full transformations at will, not beholden to only the fullness of Mother Moon like those of us that have been turned.

The only thing Endre rarely talks about is his past. He becomes silent and secretive whenever the topic is broached, and you quickly learn not to prod him with these sort of questions. No one in the pack knows exactly how old Endre is, but Lizzie claims he's been around for centuries. She says he once admitted to her that he was born in the Viking Age. He spoke of longships and pillaging and roaring across many battlefields, soaked in blood and draped in bear-fur, wielding two axes and attacking the enemies of his people with trance-like fury. He was called a berserker in those long, lost days...

Our species can be classified as quasi-immortal. We are living, breathing beings, very much alive compared to the already long dead mosquitoes. We die sooner or later, like all living things, but our lives are extended over extremely long passages of time. Human lives are candle flames compared to the lives of lycanthropes. Most of us live for centuries. There are even tales of pureborn wolves living for over a thousand years, so jaded with human life at that age that they simply abandon the guise of man-flesh forever and remain in their wolfen forms in the most remote wildernesses of the world.

I spent twelve months with the pack in the Yukon learning these things, exploring the concept of what I had become. There was a hierarchy in place within the pack, Endre the alpha, Lizzie the alpha's mate, The Twins the betas, and Raymond the lowest member, the omega. That changed when I joined the pack. I became the omega, the runt of the litter. The only one that treated me poorly because of my standing was Raymond, but that old bastard treated almost anything and anyone poorly. Most of my memories from that time period are obscenely wonderful...

Camping under the stars. Seeing the sky shimmer with greens and purples during the aurora borealis. Fishing those crystal clear rivers and hunting strong, capable moose alongside my pack mates whenever Mother Moon rose high.

Those twelve months made me fall in love with lycanthrope life. I thought if this is what remains for me in the future, then maybe all hope isn't lost after all. I wasn't alone. I was learning about the nature of my new abilities and limitations.

That's when the rumors started swirling about the upcoming time-honored tradition. Something like a lycanthropic holiday that Endre himself had created...a time for our kind to savor our role at the top of the food chain.

That's when I heard about the Feast.

That's when everything changed...

***

In the days leading up to the Feast, Endre refused to give me much information about what the tradition actually entailed. He'd simply leave me with little cryptic musings, telling me it would be a sort of "initiation" for me and I'd get to experience the full extent of what it means to live as a lycanthrope. I asked them all about it, but I met with blockages from every member of the pack. Lizzie would answer my questions with high-pitched giggles. Raymond would spit up a wad of tobacco and just grin at me with his rotting tombstone teeth. Even The Twins—typically willing to tell me almost anything—remained reluctant to divulge details of what was to come.

All they would tell me was that Endre created the Feast hundreds of years ago and the celebration was carried out once every decade or so. It's a celebration of the animal within, the opportunity to just let go and become one with the instinctual part of yourself.

What really stuck out to me were the towns and villages Jok and Thon told me about that served as Feast locations in the past. Nothing, Arizona. Dogtown, Massachusetts. Factoryville, Nebraska. The Roanoke Colony on Roanoke Island.

I was able to research them a bit later. They're all remote towns that started out with very small populations. And now? They're all ghost towns. They're listed as abandoned and forgotten, simply ruined places that are in the process of returning to nature. I even remember hearing about the Roanoke incident in elementary school. Something about a lost colony...all of the inhabitants vanishing into thin air.

I should have started putting the pieces together then, but I was willing to give my new "family" the benefit of the doubt. I figured maybe they chose ghost towns so that we could change and run and hunt without being troubled by the local population. I didn't realize that the Feast itself is what culls the populations and transforms them into ghost towns in the first place...

I savor those final days in the Yukon. Those are the only good memories I have left. Serenity captured in the pines, splashing my face in cool water from the river, the gift of being a wild thing in a wild place. That was the blissful dream before the nightmare of Old Hollow.

That was a better time before the blood, the fire, and the endless screams. It was a brief window where I was allowed to believe that our species can be peaceful monsters in the untamed spaces of the world. It was a time when I saw Endre as a charismatic leader and not bloodthirsty psychopath.

Broken memories. Lost wildernesses. Just a naïve dream before the nightmare became reality. That nightmare is very real. It's the nightmare that descended on your town. It's the nightmare that mutilated and mauled and destroyed your neighbors, your friends, and your loves ones.

Old Hollow was chosen, a meticulous, premeditated choice. Just a little nowhere town with a tiny population. A town no one remembers, a town no one even bats an eyelash at if it were to simply stop existing one day.

This nightmare is now your reality.

Your reality...is Endre's Feast.

***

Every Feast begins with the harvest moon. Endre waits for it to rise so that we'll be at our full strength, capable of complete transformations and maximum carnage. It starts with the rise of that bloated moon and we remain in the chosen town until the rise of the hunter's moon to signal the final phase and the pack's departure.

Old Hollow was chosen because of how isolated it is. It wasn't difficult for Endre and the rest of us to cut off all communication in and out of town on that first night. It was easy for us to block the only road in and out of town too.

Endre always does his homework before choosing a Feast location and he knew beforehand that Route 56 gets almost no traffic coming in aside from the handful of people that commute to work in Inwood.

Step one, pandemonium. The fires and the bullets and the serenity of the sleepy mountain hamlet turned to a war zone within minutes. That's how Endre draws most of the victims out of their homes. It's showmanship more than anything else. It's simply a baiting technique to lure the prey out into the open so that the pack can transform and then make mincemeat of the confused, groggy humans before they even realize what is happening.

That first night is centered on killing the majority of the town's inhabitants and spreading fear like a contagious virus. Endre says it like this..."when Mother Moon turns orange, we wolves turn to carnage." That's exactly what it is. Bloody, primitive carnage. The body count rises as the first few hours pass. There are little pockets of resistance here and there but these are quelled almost instantly. There's no time for the locals to organize and form even the smallest of militias to defend themselves. The element of surprise draws them out of their beds and right into the slaughterhouse streets...

And even if some considerable resistance was attempted? It would be no real threat to the pack. As most of you know by now, bullets don't stop us. They can slow us and irritate us, but they're not lethal to lycanthropes. I personally witnessed Endre walking through gunfire and taking bullet after bullet from a few roused hunters that first night, the little hunks of lead barely bee stings to him when he's in either human or wolfen form.

I wasn't prepared for that first night. I had absolutely no idea what I was walking into. The last thing I expected was a precise, full-scale massacre. Men, women, children...it didn't matter. All of them were just walking sacks of meat to Endre and the others. It was like a scene out of the darkest pit of Hell, fires burning everywhere, bodies being torn asunder, giant, baying wolves running through it all and enjoying every fateful moment.

I haven't killed anyone since I arrived in Old Hollow. As I told you, this entire horrible ordeal has been a sort of "initiation" for me. I was told to just watch the first few days. Endre said I'd get a feel for how things go, just like it's the most casual thing in the world. The others act the same way. To them, dragging a woman from her cottage by the hair and eating her alive next to her little flower garden is completely normal. The atrocities I witnessed that first night are seared into my brain forever. This is what I've become? This is what I'm expected to do?

I wish I could tell you all right now that my hands are clean. They're not. They're just as grimy as the ragged claws of the other pack members. I haven't killed anyone, but I helped to start a few of those fires in what I hoped were empty homes. I've helped to move corpses to the den that's been erected in the salvage yard. I've done things I consider unforgivable, things that fill me up with guilt that has left a permanent stain on whatever remains of my soul.

All because I wanted to fit in. All because I thought existence wouldn't be so lonely and alienating if I followed along with others like me, even becoming a member of their tattered little family.

I regret ever meeting Endre on that barren beach. My association with him has damned me. I know that in my heart, like a cold, hard lump that has become wedged inside of me. I can't continue to be a silent follower. They say you can't choose the hand that life deals you, but you can at least try to do something to change it. I'm telling you people all of this because you deserve to know the truth. You're entitled to have the facts about what is happening here. This is a warning from the lowly omega, the guy who fell in with the wrong crowd and remained under the spell of a savage alpha that has not even a streak of humanity left inside of him.

The Feast ends with the hunter's moon. It's the final night the pack will be in Old Hollow. It's the night when all of the pack members can fully transform once again—not like the partial transformations you saw some of them take advantage of at the chapel. If it reaches that point, the few remaining people in this town will have no chance whatsoever. Endre will perform his last sweep, cleansing the area of all living humans and bringing the corpses to an enormous pile that he's built up in the den.

On that final night with Mother Moon in her hunter's phase, Endre and the others will devour every single corpse on that pile while in wolfen form. It's the closing of the time-honored tradition, the last great supper before the Feast concludes for another ten years. After that, the pack leaves, and your town is dead.

At some point someone will randomly drive into Old Hollow and notice that all the people are gone. There will be no traces of them at all. Every drop of blood will be lapped up and every fragment of bone will be eaten and digested. All that dumfounded visitor will find is a town that has been abandoned, the entire population seeming to have vanished into thin air.

Just another ghost town that nobody notices or gives much thought to. A minor mystery that will never be solved, much like the lost Roanoke Colony from ages ago.

If you people remain here when the hunter's moon rises, Endre and the others will find you, kill you, and swallow down the very fact that you ever existed behind gates of serrated teeth.

21

Asher

There's a lengthy silence in the inner vault of the library after the boy stops talking. No one seems keen to break it, a heavy atmosphere hanging over the entire contingent of survivors. Luther is gaping at Grady, Vic is scrubbing at the back of his head with one hand, and Mallory is just clinging even tighter to her daughter after this chilling monologue.

Finally I gather up enough mental fortitude to respond.

"I wish I could say something to debunk what Grady has just told us, but after witnessing what happened in front of that chapel, I don't think any of us can afford to be skeptical about this."

Vic is looking about wild-eyed, his gruff voice flowing out to ooze across the room.

"How can we trust this dirty devil? He's one of them. He just admitted to it. He's been running with them a long time now. He's got that same damn yellow glow in his eyes as the rest of these fuckin' mad dogs."

Vic sits down heavily into one of the wooden chairs, allowing his head to just thump backwards against a book shelf as his eyes stare up at the overhead lights.

"Werewolves. Old Hollow being eaten up by fuckin' werewolves...what the hell kinda world is this that we're living in?" The question just seems to trail off, all of Vic's breath leaving his mouth in an exasperated sigh.

Grady simply remains sitting, his hands clasped between his legs. The boy looks extremely tired. Tired of the events happening in this town—maybe even tired of life in general.

"You said this Feast ends with the rising of the hunter's moon. Any idea how many days we have until then?"

"Three days. I know that because it's like a lunar calendar etched in my blood, a sort of internal clock," says Grady, the boy staring deeply into my eyes to emphasize the importance of his words. "On that night, everyone left in this town will die."

Mallory speaks up now, her hands running through her little girl's long, tangled hair.

"Can we get out of town before then? Just squeeze past that eighteen wheeler blocking the road and make a run for it?"

Grady sighs, shaking his head slightly.

"I wish it was that easy, ma'am. Endre will pick up the scent before you've even made it a half a mile out of town. He and the others will track you and drag you back before you even get within shouting distance of the next town. The result will be the same. Bloodshed."

The boy's voice sounds haunted, almost mechanical, as though it physically hurts him to give us this terrible news.

"You said that you and the others are quasi-immortal. You said bullets won't kill members of the pack. What about what happened in the general store? I killed one with nothing more than a heavy book..." asks Mallory, imploring Grady to give her something hopeful in turn.

"That's because you found our one weakness. It's a death sentence to lycanthropes, even pureborns. We recover from all wounds, but those inflicted by silver do lasting damage. Silver is poison for our species."

I pace back and forth for a few moments before turning to stand close to Grady while placing both palms down across the table in the center of the vault.

"There's a chance, then. If we manage to secure a few silver weapons for ourselves, we can fight these things. We can drive them out of Old Hollow before the hunter's moon even has a chance to rise. Is it possible, Grady?"

The boy seems to gather his thoughts, his eyes sweeping around the room. They linger on Cara, a sadness misting over his gaze as he thinks about what might befall the child if things go as planned in the final days of the Feast.

"It's possible with one single exception. You'd have a fighting chance against Lizzie and The Twins. They're stuck in human form until the next full moon, capable only of partial turns. They're extremely dangerous even during partial turns, but silver would even up the odds."

I can feel a sudden change overtaking the room. Some of the desperation is slipping away, a small beam of hope starting to filter over the faces of the remaining survivors.

"What's the exception?"

"Endre. You have to fully understand what you're up against when it comes to Endre. He's a pureborn. He can transform whenever he pleases. He is a giant, roaring tank composed of teeth and claws...nearly unstoppable. He is an apex predator that has lived on this planet for hundreds of years. Even with silver, getting close enough to Endre to use it is just next to impossible. You'd get shredded before you were even within range."

Some of the hope is fading. I can almost taste it fading, that familiar darkness flooding back in to replace it, a greedy, gleeful darkness. Grady is reaching into the back pocket of his jeans. Vic tenses up, but Grady simply pulls out two thin leather gloves and places them over the bare skin of his hands. He then reaches deeper into his pocket and pulls out some object wrapped in black cloth. He places it on the table, all eyes in the room seizing on the hidden item.

"None of you could get close to him. But...maybe I can."

The boy closes his eyes, breathing deeply through his nose for a moment. He carefully unfolds the cloth, showcasing a large pocketknife with a gleaming silver blade. Grady seems reluctant to even look at the blade, giving us the idea that even gazing upon it for too long irritates his eyes.

"I bought this at a little tackle shop during my last days in Nome. It was before Endre took me to meet the rest of the pack in the Yukon. I wanted it for very selfish reasons. I wanted to know I had an out if ever this curse I'm now inflicted with got to be unbearable. My plan was to keep it on my person at all times, and if the burden of living with this beast inside of me ever got to be too much, I could simply drive the blade into my temple as hard as possible and put a permanent end to things. I always planned to use this on myself...but if I can get close enough to Endre, within range of that black heart that beats in his chest...I can put it to an even better use."

Grady takes up the knife in his leather-clad hands, unfolding it and showing the others that long, sharp blade. It catches the light, the silver finish flickering with the promise of future impalement.

"I can't change what I am. I can't atone for the things I've done. It's too late for forgiveness and it's too late for me, but it's not too late for you people. If I bury this blade into Endre's chest then all that he's built will fall apart. His pack will scatter to the four winds. His Feast will become nothing but a dark, bloody memory...and you'll have your fighting chance."

I look down at the blade before lifting my eyes to take in the boy's shining face. He seems almost to see something in me, almost like he marks me as the "alpha" of this group of survivors. His eyes beg of me. His eyes crave even the barest sliver of redemption.

"Let me do this, Asher. Let me help you and your people in the only way that I can. I'll return to the den and I'll embrace Endre as my alpha one last time before giving him this sharp, toxic gift."

I look around the room to get some measure of how the others are taking this, but all eyes remain on me for some final say, any kind of permanent decision. It's on my shoulders now. The life of this boy—this boy torn unknowingly from his own humanity and thrust into a world of wolves and howling madness—now lying in my hands and sealed with whatever response I give him.

"Let me kill Endre Calder."

The silence lingers. No one in the vault dares to move. Everyone looks at me as they wait for some kind of acknowledgement. My own eyes are locked on the boy, his earnest face, his tortured need to deliver himself and other innocents from a nightmare he never asked for.

All eyes remain on me as I offer Grady a decisive nod.

22

Survivors

Grady stands facing Asher, the two men locked in a sort of desperate understanding. Grady has placed the silver blade back into the confines of his pocket, taking special care to keep his bare hands from touching any surface of the knife. The ragged little band of survivors stand behind Asher, all of them watching this final interaction between a hermit from the hills and a young man who just happens to be a werewolf.

It's surreal, but it clearly showcases that you can never judge a book by its cover. People have depths within them that can go unexplored if nobody bothers to peer beyond the surface. For Asher it's the strength behind the isolation, and for Grady it's the humanity blended with the animalism. Both men outcasts in their own way, eyes haunted, hearts heavy, so much riding on the next few hours—lives literally hanging in the balance.

"Are you sure you want to do this?" asks Asher.

"It's not a question of want, Asher. I need to do this. It's the one glimmer of hope we have. I need to separate myself from Endre and bring some kind of closure to all of this. I've been a silent party to his atrocities here for longer than I care to even admit," says Grady, the boy hanging his head slightly. "I'm the only one that can get close enough to him to carry out a swift assassination. No one in this room—myself included—can hang with Endre in a fight; whether he's in human form or wolfen form. The element of surprise is the one advantage I have over him."

"It seems so risky, Grady. What happens if he suspects that you're no longer loyal to him?"

Mallory's question just hangs for a moment, Grady letting a deep breath exhale out past his lips.

"Then it's over for me. It's a risk I'm willing to take, though. I will never be free of Endre and his influence unless I do this. I could just walk way, but he would hunt me to ends of this earth just to prove a point. Endre deals in death, always has. He won't stop until his bones are dust, his legacy carried off in the wind. It falls to me to execute that legacy..."

"How the fuck are we supposed to trust you, kid? I'm betting the first chance you get, you run outta here and go tattle to your big bad alpha about the walking bags of lunchmeat hiding out down in the yonder library," Vic snarls, his hands planted on his hips while glaring at Grady with his hard, stubborn eyes.

"Vic, if I wanted you and your people dead, then you'd be gristle strewn across the floor already. You know what I am. You know what I'm capable of. I'm not aiming to hurt you. I'm aiming to *help* you."

Asher steps forward, placing a firm hand on Vic's shoulder, managing to cool down the hothead just a little. Asher turns to Grady, his gaze solemn.

"What can we do, Grady? I believe in my heart that you're steadfast about ending Endre's existence, but what about the others? Won't they swarm you when it's done? We can help," says Asher, trying hard to make the boy understand that he's not alone in this fight. Mallory speaks up as well, joining her voice in support of this.

"You saw what I was able to do to that piece of vermin named Raymond, Grady. We might be just flesh and blood people, nothing but mortals, but we can defend ourselves. We can bring the fight to these monsters right along with you."

Grady seems reluctant to answer, the boy obviously weighing in his mind the pros and cons of this.

"Lizzie and The Twins won't stick around Old Hollow long after Endre falls, but they're still dangerous on their own without their alpha's guidance. If you mean to face them, you'll need silver. Lots of silver..."

Suddenly Luther's eyes light up, the old man rising up from his chair and letting his gaze flick from face to face.

"Edna Wicker's house. Edna's husband was a silversmith before he died. Martin and I were friends years and years ago, we used to drink lemonade on the porch and talk about the old times. That house is full of all manner of silver tools. There are knives, pots and pans, utensils, even specialty items that people used to bring to Martin for repairs. It's a veritable arsenal."

Once again, that wispy sense of hope comes alive in the vault. There's a chance. There's a plan taking shape. These bedeviled souls see the faintest glow of light beyond a tunnel that squirms with claws and teeth and yellow-tinted eyes.

"There's an abandoned apartment complex that's right next to the salvage yard. It's four stories of sturdy brick, the windows on the upper floor sure to provide a bird's eye view of this "den" that's been constructed below. We can gather as many silver weapons as we can from Edna's house. We can lie in wait there, just watching, and when Endre is dispatched we'll descend on that salvage yard and help you fend off the rest of the pack," says Asher. "Just another element of surprise that works in our favor, Grady."

Grady seems to consider all of this, the boy lightly nibbling on his bottom lip as he thinks of the implications of such an assault.

"It'll have to be tonight. It'll be dark soon and Endre will start to wonder where Raymond and I are. If we do this, we go all in. We don't have the luxury of a practice run. No second chances available. We succeed...or we die."

"We will succeed. Mallory and Luther, you two stay here to keep Cara safe behind the vault door. Vic and I will go to the silversmith's house to gather as many weapons as we can. We'll wait in one of the abandoned apartments on the fourth floor. We'll wait until that blade is buried in the albino's heart and then we'll ambush the others. It'll be three on three then. Those are favorable odds, the best odds we've had since all of this started," says Asher, casting his eyes on all the people in the room. Luther and Mallory give their assent to remain behind, Cara being a priority that all of the survivors want to keep safe at all costs.

The survivors talk a little longer. The plan grows and evolves. Hope grows with it—like a small plant after a draught.

23

Grady's Goodbye

Mallory hugs the boy close, whispering into his ear a heartfelt thank you. Luther nods to him, and Cara offers a little wave to the strange boy with the eyes that sometimes shine like her yellow crayons.

Asher and Vic follow Grady out of the vault, Mallory and Luther remaining behind with Cara. Mallory stops Asher on his way out the circular entrance, her hand reaching forward to graze against his own. He lets their fingers interlock for a moment, nothing being said between them, just a lingering glance.

"Come back."

"We will..."

Asher reluctantly breaks away, watching as Luther and Mallory work together to close the vault door. The three of them walk through the lobby, stopping at the main entrance with Grady turning to them.

"Once you two have made it into the house of the silversmith and gathered weapons, I'll make my move on Endre. I'll wait behind the fountain across the street from the apartment complex. You'll need to signal me somehow from one of the windows."

Asher thinks for a moment before reaching into his pocket and pulling out his butane lighter. He flicks it into life, the flame dancing and flickering, painting the faces of the trio with twisting shadows. Twilight reigns outside, the muddled dimness of day becoming night.

"I'll wave the flame in the window facing the street. You'll be able to see it in the dark and they won't be able to see it from the salvage yard."

Grady swallows, nodding solemnly.

They say no more. There is nothing left but to walk through the gathering dark, their footsteps light across asphalt, the men all believing in their hearts that they're walking willingly into peril. It has to be done. It's what's right. Resistance...

24

Asher

We leave Grady crouching behind the fountain, the boy seeming frail next to the large spouting structure. Numerous pennies gleam beneath the clear water of the fountain, the head of a carved cherub spraying the water upwards in a lazy arch. Grady reaches into the water and cups his hands together, taking a deep drink. He looks like what he is at this moment in time. Just a boy. Just a youth that shouldn't have to be entangled in this desperate plan to overthrow an otherworldly tyrant.

Life can be so cruelly unpredictable at times. Edna's house is barely half a block from the fountain, and it'll be dark by the time we put together our own personal arsenals. I can't help but stare at that looming salvage yard in the distance, fenced and distant now, but the threat that lies behind the barrier eating at all three of us.

"You need to go."

The boy is right. Time is pivotal here and Endre will expect Raymond and Grady to return soon. If they linger, Endre might lead the pack out to search the town for them. That would be very bad for all parties involved.

"We'll be back soon. I'll use the lighter from that window..."

I point to one of the grimy windows near the top floor of the derelict apartment building. Grady nods. Vic shifts on his feet uncomfortably, his work boots dusty and battered.

"Look for knives. Look for bludgeoning weapons. Anything that you know for a fact is forged silver."

Grady taps a hand against his own chest.

"When the time comes, you aim whatever you find at their hearts. It's the surest way."

I'm reluctant to leave the boy there, but time continues to haunt us. Vic and I start down the road, cutting through yards and parking lots. I look back once, just making out Grady's silhouetted form taking another drink from the fountain.

25

Asher

A part of me hoped that we'd find Edna hiding away safe inside of her cottage. There's no sign of the old woman aside from her spectacles lying in the yard. They're broken and smeared in drying maroon beneath the old tire swing, the ropes of the swing creaking lightly in the breeze, seeming to greet Vic and I with a hopeless, lonely sound. We don't have to struggle to gain entry to the house because the front door stands wide open, a gaping maw just begging for visitors.

I move cautiously ahead with Vic close behind me. It's clear that a great struggle occurred in the home, lamps and knickknacks lying shattered across the floor. A door near the back of the cottage was literally bashed off the hinges, now leaning precariously against a washing machine with ragged claw marks descending down the exterior surface.

The wolves have been here...and it seems apparent that they glutted themselves on the sole occupant.

"Poor old Edna. She would have lived to be a hundred, I just know it. I remember how she used to give me black licorice when I was just a punk kid riding my bike home from school," Vic trails off, shaking his head at the sheer inhumanity on display in the rubble of the old woman's house.

"These animals have no compassion, Vic. It's time we showed them that they fucked with the wrong town..."

I motion Vic forward, both of us moving deeper down a narrow hallway near the side of the cottage. I push the door at the end of the corridor open and the room seems to shimmer in front of me, my eyes catching upon so many objects that gleam and catch the light. It's Martin's workshop, shelves piled high with silver objects of all shape and size, even a variety of items hanging from hooks and racks along the walls.

"Shitfire, Asher...looks like we hit the mother lode."

"Can't argue that..."

Vic is already bustling forward, jamming his jacket pockets with shining knives and seizing upon a dog's head cane made of forged silver. He holds up the cane, turning it over and examining the craftsmanship with a lopsided grin.

"I call dibs on this beauty. These wolves like to bite...well Ol' Scrappy here likes to bite right back."

"Really, Vic? Ol' Scrappy?"

I can't help but chuckle at Vic naming the cane, my own hands busy securing several silver hunting blades into a black vest that was draped over a stool in the corner. I slide the vest over my body, liking the weight of the concealed blades within. It's a little tight on me, but it'll serve. Meanwhile Vic is rummaging through a cabinet drawer, taking up handfuls of sterling silver rings and shoving them into the pockets of his pants.

"We can smelt these down, make bullets outta them, ya know?"

"I don't know that we'll have the time or the resources to do that."

Vic scoffs, proceeding to place a few of the larger rings onto his thick fingers and then balling up his fist for me to see.

"Well, if not, they still make damn good brass knuckles..."

That idea isn't half bad, so I simply shrug and smile in response. My attention is captured by a hatchet with a gleaming finish, the blade cut to a keen perfection. I pick up the hatchet, taking a moment to gaze at my own reflection in the polished silver. My beard is a little scruffier than usual, my eyes haunted by dark circles. I slide the hatchet into my belt and do another slow circle around the workshop.

"We've gotta get going, Vic. You all armored up?"

I finally turn to face him. He's removed a large cloth from a statuesque figure in a darkened corner of the workshop, gaping up at it with his mouth hanging open.

"Speaking of armor..."

Vic is staring up at a full suit of medieval armor crafted from silver, obviously some collector's item that a patron had commissioned shortly before Martin's death. I can't help but marvel at the armor as well, the detail work of the grated helmet, the gauntlets looking especially impressive with ribbed metalwork. It seems Martin only had time to finish the upper torso portion of the suit, the lower body missing.

"Temping, Sir Lancelot...but we have to move."

Vic finally shakes himself out of his stupor, both of us giving that incredible armor a final look.

"Yeah. Let's roll."

We make for the door, both of us outfitted with a variety of silver weaponry. Hopefully it'll give us the edge we need...

***

It doesn't take us long to get back to the street, and we nod at Grady from the entrance of the old apartment building. He offers us a little halfhearted wave in response. I push through a boarded up window that enters into the lobby, and both Vic and I are just able to scramble through.

This old building has been here for as long as I can remember, a local spot that everyone considers haunted. It stinks of mildew and decaying wood, the walls covered in graffiti and empty liquor bottles lying strewn across the floor.

The staircase is rickety as hell, but it bears the weight of both of us as Vic and I climb our way up to the fourth floor. The air in the complex is stagnant, little puffs of dust trailing down from the ceiling as we work our way up higher and higher.

For the briefest moment I think I hear some kind of drifting whisper coming from one of the apartment doors we pass on the third floor. The words come muffled from behind a thick wooden door with the letter "M" carved into it. Vic seems to sense it too, shivering against icy tendrils that creep from beneath the door's threshold. I keep us moving forward, shaking my head. The last thing we need is to let ghostly imaginings creep into our minds when lives are at stake.

Finally we reach the fourth floor, Vic shouldering through a door into a barren little apartment. I head over to the window overlooking the salvage yard, a ratty curtain still obscuring most of the view. I'm careful to move this aside only an inch or two so that I can see out of the window. The salvage yard is dark aside from a raging bonfire in the center, the flames mostly hidden by stacks of stripped automobiles. My eyes linger on the enormous pile of corpses near that fire. It's a sight that sears itself into my mind, almost all the inhabitants of Old Hollow nude and dismembered, strewn across that pile like nothing but hunks of butchered meat.

Vic takes a look through the curtain on the opposite side, a little hiss escaping from his teeth.

"Sick fuckin' freaks."

It takes a great deal of willpower to pull myself from that hideous sight, but I know time is slipping away from us. I head over to the window that overlooks the street and the fountain below. This is the moment we've all been building towards. Once it starts, there's no stopping it...

I raise up the butane lighter and give it a flick, the orange flame burning bright against the grimy surface of the window. The boy rises down there near the fountain. The boy meets my eyes from across distance and dirty glass, and I still manage to see the conviction that burns in his gaze.

Grady begins walking towards the salvage yard. Old Hollow's new mouth of Hell, all twisted metal teeth and fire-lashing tongue. The boy never looks back.

26

Alpha & Omega

Grady trudges across the hard dirt of the salvage yard, his eyes momentarily drifting up to the fenced entrance and the razor wire strung up above. This landscape of ruin is like a maze, a labyrinth constructed of obsolete objects and dead, abandoned things. He weaves through narrow aisles, stacks of crushed automobiles looming on either side of him like towering walls. He feels slightly claustrophobic, little droplets of sweat beading across his temples, this entire world of ravaged metal and filth seeming to press in on him from all sides.

Still he continues onward, the weight of his dreadful work swirling in his mind. The silver knife is tucked into a leather band strapped to his lower back beneath his t-shirt, several pieces of stripped cloth keeping the silver from touching his bare skin and agitating it. He must be quick when he draws the knife. He must get close, so intimately close, and he must be quicker than he has ever been in all of his years. It all hinges on that single thrust. He mustn't stop for anything. He must make himself deaf to Endre's charming words. He must be numb, a living weapon, his purpose to cut out the heart of a pallid serpent that has lived for far too long...

His breath plumes from his mouth as the sun sinks fully behind North Mountain, the air taking on a lingering chill. Books lie rotten and waterlogged all around him. Bicycles rusted and heaped onto junk piles, their riders lost to the annals of time. Plastic dolls watch his progress, their dresses tattered, their eyes smeared in mud. No child will ever pick them up again. This is a bad place, a sad place. Grady feels that in his heart, but still he walks on. The wolves have nested in this axis of decay. Wolves he once called his brethren—now just ravenous murderers that intend to kill what remains of this town and strangle the last little slivers of life from it.

Endre's damned Feast. His vision of the world, to hunt, to kill, to pillage and consume all that stands before him. There's no room for remembered humanity in Endre's crusade. You either embrace the beast or you feed the beast. There is no middle ground. There is only Alpha, the ragged king, the pale eater of eons, and all those that would run at his heels like willing, subservient hounds.

Grady is the lowest of them. The Omega, last on the totem pole, the bottom of the wolfen hierarchy. Still he winds through corridors of smeared and forgotten things, the stench of corpses and firewood drawing him towards his destiny.

Omega meets Alpha. The boy, newly turned, against a lycanthrope that has walked this world since the days of the ancient Norsemen. Grady must not falter. He must be swift, his aim true.

Most of all, he must remember the worth of the humanity that still sputters within his animal-infected soul.

***

The bonfire welcomes Grady with rising cinders and curling smoke, that infamous mountain of festering corpses rising up behind it like a scene out of the lowest pit of Tartarus. The pack is gathered around the great fire, each of them seeming quiet, caught up in their own little ruminations. Lizzie sits curled up in the lap of a fresh cadaver, the man's face draped with a ratty white sheet, blood droplets bleeding through to stain the material. She's doodling on the shrouded face with a black marker, sketching out blackened vines from the man's sunken eye sockets. She hums while she does this, lightly tapping her combat boots together. Grady walks past her, and she offers the boy a familiar giddy smile. Her face so infinitely beautiful, those turquoise eyes the only sign of the madness that crawls beneath the surface.

The Twins seem reflective as well, the two of them working on some dripping sculpture on the other side of the bonfire. It's a kind of tribal art born from the hands of the Dinka hunters, multiple coiled human spinal cords twisted and braided together around the dull metal of a flagpole, the skulls still connected to the cords and hanging downward, jaws unhinged and gaping towards the soil.

They nod a greeting to Grady and then return to their artistic endeavors, the boy's boots carrying him around the fire to the figure that sits beneath the mountain of the dead.

Endre is stretched out on a large seat ripped out from a charter bus, the leather torn and ravaged, the giant albino looming there like a primeval king on an improvised throne. His wild white hair flows against his shoulders in the breeze, the firelight playing in the pinkish hues of his eyes. He gnaws at a bone, something pulled from the mountain behind him—the spoils of his Feast. His teeth tear at meat, stretching it out until the flesh rips clean and vanishes into his maw.

Endre says nothing as Grady approaches. He simply chews, watching the boy. The silence lasts between Alpha and Omega, just the crackling fire at their backs and the lightest wind teasing at their hair.

Finally the Alpha breaks the tension with his words.

"You've been gone awhile. I was starting to worry..."

"Yeah, it's my bad, Endre. Ray and I got caught up searching for stragglers. We kinda lost track of time. Ray is checking one last house...he sent me on ahead. He should be back soon."

Endre nods, taking another bite from the bone. A droplet of pinkish blood runs along the porcelain flesh of his chin.

"Find anyone?"

Grady shakes his head, his hands rising to rest on his hips. He hopes very much that Endre doesn't notice how nervous he is. He knows Endre can smell the sweat in his pores, but can he smell a lie too?

"Not a soul. We think maybe it was just scent from the church that the breeze carried down the road."

Endre lets his tongue slip out, licking across the calcified surface of the bone. It looks like a humerus, long and pitted, once a living being's arm.

"That's a shame. I know a few cattle remain in town. It's just a matter of smoking them out. We can wait until Mother Moon rises again before we do that...her hunter's face will soon shine bright."

Grady nods while swallowing, Endre reaching up behind him to pull down a hunk of flesh from a decaying torso balanced on the mountain of the dead. He holds this out in his pallid palm, an offering for the Omega. It would be an insult to refuse it.

"I know I've been hard on you, Grady. I understand this is all a lot to take in for a newly blooded pup. This isn't the Eden that the Yukon was for us, but it's a garden all the same. Old Hollow blooms with flesh and blood, and all of it is ours for the picking. You've gotta open your eyes and forget what it was like to be among the cattle, just fearful prey lost in the herd..."

Endre beckons Grady forward, and the boy has no choice but to come. The meat smells good. The boy could eat of it and do exactly what Endre is asking of him. He could forsake humanity. He could turn his back on the people he promised to save.

"You're the wolf at the herd's heels now, boy. It takes a little tough love to hammer that in, but that's all it is. Centuries await us, Grady. Claim this meat...and eat of my Feast. Be what you are. Be guiltless about what you are..."

Endre's words seem so hypnotic, so deliciously charming. The scent of the "cattle" flesh is in Grady's nostrils now, intoxicating him, drawing him forward. The wolf within slavers for it. The man within screams out against it, but his voice is distant and small; the wolf's baying overriding the pleas.

Grady is walking toward Endre's throne beneath the mountain of the defiled dead. His eyes have yellowed, his heart hammering in his chest. This is the defining moment of his destiny. He feels that in every part of himself, this little fractured piece of night seeming to play out for him in a slow, timeless reel. Endre leans forward even more, reaching forward, offering that meat like the serpent offered the apple in long lost Eden.

Grady's left hand is extending, the fingers digging into the offering of meat, sour blood squelching out from his grip. He takes a final step forward, his body mere inches from Endre's own. He can smell the Alpha—the scents of the apex predator—smoke from the bonfire, gristles of meat in his teeth, the mingling aroma of vast wildernesses and unfathomable strength. Their eyes meet. Grady's gleaming yellowish orbs, Endre's red rubies set within his skull.

It all happens so fast. Grady feels the compassion rising above the hunger. He feels the battle within himself reaching a conclusion, the beast wrestled to the ground by the good man he desperately wants to be. It has to be now.

The boy reaches around to his lower back and claims the blade there, the hilt wrapped in strands of protective cloth. Still locked in the endless scarlet eyes of his Alpha, the boy whips his balled fist around and makes sure his thrust is clean. The silver blade moves so swiftly, whistling through the air, the speed of it mesmerizing as it heads towards the scarred chest where the beating heart lies.

The tip of the blade pierces that ivory skin...but something stops it from sinking deeper. A pallid hand shot up at the last possible second, those fingers now wrapped around the blade, tendrils of steam rising from the flesh as it's seared from the effect of the silver. Endre has not broken eye contact with the boy. He does not release the blade, managing to just endure the burning pain. The albino sighs deeply while rising from his throne, his great shadow falling over Grady.

He casually pulls the blade from his chest—a mere centimeter wound lurking there—before tossing it to the soil at Grady's feet. The boy is frozen. Grady becomes vaguely aware that the others are watching, Jok and Thon looking on with mild disappointment. Lizzie plays at the shroud of her cadaver, plucking at the sheet with her fingertips.

Endre's voice is like Death's bony hand caressing the boy's cheek, so soft, so final.

"You were dead the moment you walked back into this den, Grady. Every step, every word—just a game leading to the gallows. Show him, Lizzie..."

Endre casually motions with one hand to Lizzie, and the madwoman sweeps the sheet from the cadaver, revealing the identity of the body. It's Raymond, his face squashed to pulp, a few tendrils of dried chewing tobacco still smeared across his mouth. The boy's head sinks, his heart sinking with it. He was careless.

"I can forgive many things, boy...but betrayal is not one of them. You've been trafficking with cattle, playing house with prey. The stink of them saturates you..."

Grady's eyes shimmer gold, his claws sprouting and his teeth elongating. The bestial side sings in his blood, but the fear he feels is purely human. It went wrong. It went irrevocably wrong…

"My little Judas Iscariot wearing a sheep suit in a circle of wolves. You had potential, boy. You could have walked this world with me for hundreds of years, a devourer of nations. Why throw it all away for worthless cattle in a doomed stockyard?"

The boy forces himself to meet the eyes of the Alpha. He sets his jaw, his voice carrying so much conviction that the sound of it surprises him.

"They're not cattle. They're *people*. People with hearts and souls, things you lost lifetimes ago. You and this pack of killers will never grasp the meaning of that."

The boy pauses, staring defiant daggers into the albino's blazing eyes. Endre simply smiles, his grin toothy and wide.

"Take solace in the fact that once it's over, I won't eat you, Grady. I'll leave your carcass to the flies…"

All talking ceases with Endre's pallid fist ascending upwards, catching the boy on the underside of the chin. The impact instantly shatters his jaw, his teeth clattering together, many of them breaking off in his mouth. His body flies through the air before crashing down into the dust before the bonfire.

The boy coughs against the dirt, struggling to rise up and fight. His eyes catch on The Twins and they look away from him. Lizzie just titters. There will be no help from the pack. He's the lone wolf now, driven out and driven low. Endre comes for him again, the boots beginning to fall, crushing down against Grady's ribs, stomps that shatter bone and puncture organs almost instantly.

A pale hand reaches down and lifts the boy up by his t-shirt, his body rising into the air like he's nothing but a very small child. Endre reaches into the bonfire and he retrieves a burning log, and he proceeds to pivot on his heels and *crush* the flaming log into Grady's sternum with all the power he can muster. The boy flies through the air like he was just hit by an eighteen wheeler truck, his body smashing up against a rusted military convoy vehicle, the impact creating a deep crater of obliterated metal in the shape of Grady's broken form.

Breathing is hard now for the boy. His insides are full of sharp protrusions and crumbled bones. Blood leaks down from his head, a portion of his scalp torn away, just filleted skin drooping against his face with plasma running into his eyes. He watches the Alpha coming for what is left of him through a red haze. He tries to move his head when Endre picks up the silver blade from the ground, but his spinal cord is severed and his limbs don't seem to work properly anymore.

The boy thinks of Seattle, that clean air and the endless rainfall that used to kiss his skin. He thinks of sunsets in Alaska, the ocean stretching out before him like the end of the earth. He remembers nights at the bar, girls in pretty dresses, and the smell of those evergreen trees in the wilds of the Yukon. He thinks of anything but the monster stomping towards him.

He summons the last of his strength to raise his ruined head up towards that apartment building in the distance. He looks to the windows on the top floor. His whisper is dry, just words barely formed on lips.

"I'm sorry. I tried. Run..."

The boy barely feels it as the blade drags across his throat, slashing open flesh and veins, his blood bubbling out of him like corrosive acid from the poisonous effect of the silver.

The life flows out of him slowly, staining the dirt at his feet. His eyes become glassy, the bonfire becoming a blur, the albino fading from sight, a darkness surrounding him like the canopy of many tall trees.

The last thing he smells are evergreens in a far away forest...

***

The turn comes in the heart of fury, Endre's vocal cords unleashing a bloodcurdling howl before he's even fully transformed into his wolfen shape. He takes a few swipes at the boy's face, clawing away features, identity, and the Omega's very existence.

He inhales deeply of the air, his muzzle flaring. The eyes of the Alpha trail across the den, taking in that apartment building across from the far fence. He glares at The Twins, his lips peeling back from massive canines. His voice comes out in a murderous bark, syllables formed of growls.

"Cattle aided him in his treachery. I smell their fear, their anger, and a petulant desire for vengeance..."

The great white wolf extends a paw towards the top floor of the building, pointing out the covered windows.

"Fetch them. Let them say a prayer over the traitor's corpse while I piss on it."

The Twins race off towards the building, their movements lithe. Endre and Lizzie stay near Grady's remains. The Alpha leans against the wrecked military convoy, raising up one leg and letting the yellow stream of urine flow out to saturate and defile the boy's shredded face.

The Alpha grins up at the apartment windows as he does this. The Twins will bring forth the coconspirators. Oh, how they'll bleed...

27

Asher

The world seems soundless. I'm vaguely aware that I'm roaring out words, my entire body straining against Vic's firm grip. I'm not sure what I'm saying. I'm just reaching towards that window, the cords standing out across my neck, little specks of saliva flying from my mouth.

We watched what happened in front of the bonfire. We watched Grady being flung around down there like a rag doll. I didn't see him die, but I felt it, a scalloping sensation in the lowest pit of my gut. A few old automobile husks fell to the wayside just in time for us to see the albino desecrating Grady's corpse, urinating on the ruined remains while pointing up at this very window.

The boy risked it all for people he didn't even know—just something in his heart that told him the bloodshed must end. He died trying to right a wrong he wasn't even responsible for. I grieve for him for only the briefest moment, but that grief turns to molten rage as the pale bastard down there showers his frail body with piss. I want to kill him. I want his shaggy head on a plate with silver forks driven through those wretched red eyes...

Sound returns, my eardrums popping. Vic is desperately trying to communicate with me, his face frantic, his arms waving as he points downwards in the direction of the staircase we ascended. I hear it now. The sound of footfalls slamming up those stairs, wolves on the hunt, wolves coming to finish the job. Vic pulls me towards the apartment door, dragging me towards a sagging exit that leads to the rooftop of the building. I finally regain some semblance of composure, both of us stumbling out past the ribbed industrial piping, our feet carrying us across the tarred roof.

Those footfalls are louder behind us in the stairwell, gaining, feet impacting wood so hard that I can practically envision the splinters flying. We run to the edge of the rooftop, a rusty terrace descending downward on the other side of the building. It's the only way down, the solitary escape route. Vic pushes me towards it, his hand pointing towards the library across town.

It's all happening so fast, but it seems like time has slowed down as well. The sound of our pursuers is close, dangerously close.

I gaze into Vic's face. The mercurial man that I met when all of this began is barely there now, replaced by someone who has risen to his fullest potential in the depths of tragedy. There's something noble about his features in the shadows of the rooftop, his mouth a hard line that dominates his face. He speaks to me, but I barely hear it, my ears still ringing from the event we just witnessed in the salvage yard. I read his lips, the words seeming to drift towards me across the expanse of some great cave.

"Save them."

There's no time to argue. There's no time to say goodbye. Sometimes in life the one thing you wish for most of all is just more time, but time is cruel, and the clock turns backs for no one. I nod, swallowing deeply. I cannot let his sacrifice be in vain. I scramble down the terrace, my hands gripping slippery railing, little specks of rust drifting down into my hair.

The last sound I hear before my feet hit the ground is the rooftop door smashing off the hinges up there.

I tear across the mangled streets with my breath burning through my lungs. I run as hard as I possibly can towards the vault. There's still time for Mallory, Cara, and Luther.

There's still time to save them.

28

Vic's Last Stand

The Twins burst through the rooftop door at the same instant, the corrugated steel bending from the hinges and literally snapping forward, the door sliding several yards across the tarred roof. They witness a solitary man standing near the far edge of the rooftop. He's doing a peculiar thing, reaching deeply into his pockets and slamming some snack into his mouth, swallowing deeply each time. Vic smacks his lips a few times, the acrid taste sliding down his throat. He grins at The Twins, beckoning them forward while twirling his dog's head cane.

The Twins lope towards him from the right and left, their eyes usually the color of dark pools of oil—now glowing like yellow lanterns fed by that same oil. Their ragged bone claws scrape against the roof's surface, their sharp teeth chattering together as they close in on their quarry. They're both in the phase that Grady called "a partial turn", all teeth and talons intent on opening Vic up like a tin can.

Jok closes in first, but Vic whips the cane to the side and catches him across the temple, the silver head of the cane stinging and knocking Jok to the side. Before Vic can continue the assault, Thon is right there, slashing out with his claws and catching Vic on the back of the knee. Vic grunts in pain, his leg buckling, and Jok recovers enough to race forward and crush a knee up against the cane, splintering the wood and sending the silver dog's head flying somewhere out of reach.

Vic makes a final attempt to rise up, but The Twins descend on him, snarling, biting—just organic killing machines that nullify his ability to fight back within seconds. He's thrown onto his back, claws sweeping down at him over and over again, bits of cloth and flesh flying as The Twins rend their victim into ribbons. Vic grits his teeth against this, struggling not to cry out. He doesn't want to give these loathsome hounds the pleasure of even a single scream.

His will is tested when The Twins sink their faces down against Vic's stomach, chewing into it, lapping up the blood that flows and snapping up pieces of muscle, sinew, and finally the pulpy organs that lie beneath. Thon slurps on Vic's lower intestine like a strand of spaghetti while Jok takes deep, hearty bites of the reddened crater of the exposed stomach. Vic feels the shock setting in, adrenal sweat bursting out across his forehead and cheeks as he's being eaten alive.

Still, he clings to life just a tiny bit longer. He manages to open his mouth, blood oozing out of it and splattering against the faces of his Dinka executioners. He speaks to them, his words bubbling from the red river of his open mouth.

"How...do I taste, fellas?"

The Twins stop dining on innards for a moment, staring up incredulously at the mutilated prey. There's a raw chugging sound coming up from the slashed remnants of his throat. He's laughing. The Sudanese hunters cock their heads at each other, uncomprehending.

"I...had a last meal. Every man on death row deserves...a...last meal, don't he?"

Vic opens up a balled fist, showing The Twins his open palm. There's a single sterling silver ring gleaming brightly there. Vic just keeps right on smiling up at Endre's betas, his grin a horrible, reddened rictus.

"One left. I ate the rest."

Vic leans his head up just slightly, taking a moment to spit a geyser of blood into the faces of both Jok and Thon. He falls back down, his dead man's laugh sinking deeply into the sensitive holes that comprise The Twin's eardrums.

"Expect a little...indigestion, you ugly fuckers..."

All light fades from Vic's eyes. He dies with that satisfied grimace still etched across his face. The Twins stare at each other for a moment, a rare look of horror dawning on those identical faces. That's when the cramps start, the consumed silver flowing through their bloodstreams, the rings lodging in their guts and poisoning them slowly. The pain is unbearable. The silver works its dark magic inside of them, snapping their veins like twine, curdling their lungs, rushing up to the heart to burn like corrosive battery acid in a failing pump. They writhe on the rooftop, shaking with seizures, little blisters popping and healing and then popping again all over their bodies, each one like a pimple that oozes metallic-colored pus.

The poisoned hunters reach for each other, brother seeking brother, the two of them sharing in their suffering just as they've shared in everything for the entirety of their lifetimes.

The Twins press their scarified foreheads together, both of them curled up into the fetal position. They're in the womb once more, but this is death's womb, and there's no comfort in the dark pinpricks that blot out their eyes.

The corrosive silver reaches their brains, cooking the gray matter within the crock pots that their skulls have become. Thon's mouth falls open and a lump of melted sterling silver falls off his tongue to click against the rooftop. Death swoops in, burning and toxic, a scythe that cleaves them from the inside out. Even their pores drip with silver perspiration...

The Twins came into this world at exactly the same time.

In a fitting twist of fate, The Twins exit this world at exactly the same time too.

29

Great White Wolf

The albino emerges onto the rooftop, trudging slowly forward in tattered jeans and road-weary boots. The crescent moon in the sky paints his face, seeming almost to reach down with a sickle hand and caress the curve of his cheek. The wind tousles his shaggy white hair, those pink-hued eyes falling upon the two dark shapes curled together in the center of the roof. It appears as though his anatomy was carved out of alabaster, all the edges hard and rough, nothing soft about his flesh, the skin having been touched by all of earth's elements for hundreds and hundreds of years.

Endre sighs, a deep, throaty sound. He crouches down next to the bodies of The Twins. Raymond meant nothing to him. He was just a stupid old mule to round out the ranks, stubborn and insipidly cruel, but easily manipulated. The Twins were different. He respected The Twins, even came to take solace in their presence at his side. His loyal Lieutenants brought down by the trickery of these increasingly brazen cattle...

Endre reaches into the back pocket of his jeans and removes a small beaten pouch. It smells infinitely old, something he picked up at a bazaar in Morocco just a few months before he found The Twins on their deathbeds in the African bush. He resurrected them then. He only wishes he could do the same now.

Pallid fingers reach into the pouch, plucking out four dried petals, the texture of them crackly, the color a deep violet. Wolfsbane harvested from some distant field centuries past when parts of the world were still young and men and women traveled by horse-drawn carriage. That field is surely gone by now, likely razed and turned into some strip mall or a hideous erection of concrete and asphalt to suit the needs of the cattle. That is how it always is. Nature paved over and ruined, the wild places dwindling with each passing day. The stink of the cattle saturates everything now, all of them breeding like mewling rats, their cities blotting out the moonlight with smog, their chemicals polluting the rivers, their careless actions slowly but surely poisoning the lushness of the world. Endre hates the cattle with every fiber of his being. They deserve culling. They deserve each and every holocaust he brings down upon them in the name of purification—his noble, cleansing Feast.

The albino gently turns Jok and Thon over, closing their tortured eyes, the dark lids seeming to just slide over those equally dark irises. He carefully places a wolfsbane petal overtop each eye. It's the closest thing the lupine species has to a funeral rite. A gift of wolfsbane for the dead, just a simple token to earn the mercy of Mother Moon.

"Go now to the Great Forest where the pines never end. Run and hunt forever, and may your bellies always be full and your spirits always free under the everlasting glow of Mother Moon."

The words are ancient, most of them coming back to his mind in the old Norse tongue. He was a beta then in a pack along the highlands of Skåne. It seems like an eternity since then. There have been many packs since. Many packs, many losses, and many Feasts.

Endre rises up from his crouched position, his scarlet eyes momentarily falling on the cattle-corpse that lies next to The Twins. A twisting rage overcomes the Alpha, serpents coiling and uncoiling in his chest. He roars out into the night, a trumpeting howl that sends bats flying fearfully from the distant streetlamps. Endre smashes down his boot on Vic's face over and over again, crushing bone and flesh, making it nothing but an unrecognizable soup of plasma and cerebrospinal fluid.

His preternatural hearing detects the loud purring of the engine being fired up in the salvage yard, Lizzie tearing out of the entrance on her Vincent Black Shadow, the madwoman guiding the motorcycle through the twisted streets like a rattling death-machine. His hellcat will find the man who's now running across the barren remnants of Old Hollow, his feet hammering pavement and his heart thudding in his chest just as loudly. Endre can hear him fleeing from the rooftop even though he's made it several blocks by now. The albino can smell the blood in his veins and the desperation oozing from his pores. Lizzie will run him down...but his death will not be quick.

His skin will be flayed. His eyes will be sucked from the sockets and popped like grapes. His fingernails will be peeled off and thrown to the bonfire. And then, when his screams rival an orchestra, he'll be roasted alive until the meat is well done. That is the price of defiance. That...is the way of the Feast.

30

Vroom Vroom

Asher's boots pound against the floor, his arms reaching up to smash into the inner library doors as he races towards the vault, his lungs like flaring sacks of flame within his chest. He calls out, his voice instantly recognizable, and Mallory and Luther pop the vault door open, Cara lingering there with her hands wrapped around her mommy's leg.

"What's happened?" asks Mallory, her fair features flushed, her eyes glittering with anxiety.

"It went bad. Endre knew about Raymond. It was a trap. Grady is dead. Vic didn't make it...we have to go, and we have to go now," says Asher, breathless and speaking in clipped sentences while struggling to usher all three of his people out of the vault. Mallory tugs along at Cara's little hand, Luther following behind, the old man's eyes seeming to flick everywhere at once.

Asher is just about to lead them towards the main entrance when the terrible sound of shattering glass explodes across the lobby, quickly followed by the ominous purr of a very powerful engine. Asher moves backwards, getting Mallory and Cara hidden behind one of the larger shelves in the fiction section. Luther stumbles behind them, crouching down with his gnarled hands braced against the steel leg of one of the shelves. Asher turns to his people, mouthing the word "quiet" while he strains to hear exactly what the new unwanted visitor is doing.

Cara notices her dropped coloring book a few feet across the aisle, the little girl darting forward to retrieve it. Mallory makes a desperate attempt to snag her shirt and drag her backwards, but Cara is too quick, her little legs pumping as she reaches a hand towards the spine of the book.

A voice pipes up from the other end of the aisle, lilting and high-pitched, the singsong words of sanity scorched into cinders.

"Mmm. Is that child-flesh Mommy smells? A wee little calf out of the corral? Mommy is ever so hungry! Mommy...wants a little veal."

The sound of the Vincent Black Shadow cruising slowly along pins Cara in place with her hand on the book, the little girl frozen in fear while staring down the corridor. Lizzie Fontaine sits atop the motorcycle like it's some horrible steed comprised of living parts and black, glistening chrome. The madwoman is a sight to behold, her dark hair hanging in ringlets and braided through with raven's feathers on one side, those turquoise eyes locking upon Cara and willing the little girl to fall into the depraved depths of them.

Lizzie's smile is equally captivating, teeth as sharp as razors and a forked tongue slipping out to toy with the tips of them.

"Hiya, kiddo. Like my pony? She's a real beauty. How about you join me for a ride? We can go to Wonderland. We can have tea and crumpets, and we can tickle that rude old caterpillar until he squeals."

Lizzie is slowly walking the bike towards Cara, her hands gripping firm to the handlebars, the tiniest tips of bone claws starting to extend outward from beneath the chipped black polish of her fingernails.

"My pony is the prettiest, isn't she? I feed her oil instead of oats. My pony doesn't say neigh like other ponies do. Can you guess what noise she makes, little girl?"

Lizzie is slowly closing the distance, Cara gaping at her, the little girl's eyes wide saucers full of terrified tears that are beginning to blur her vision.

"I'll tell you. My pony says....VROOM VROOM."

Lizzie immediately wrenches back on the throttle, a wild cackle exiting her throat as she guides the chopper down the aisle, the speed picking up and the headlamp shining, blinding Cara. The little girl holds up a forearm to block her eyes and she starts to run in the opposite direction, Lizzie in hot pursuit, the wheels of the motorcycle tearing up pieces of carpet, the stench of burning rubber making Cara cough even as she runs for her life.

Lizzie bears down on the handlebars even harder, leaning over them, screaming like a banshee as she closes in on the fleeing figure.

"Stop running, sweetie pie! I'll make a doll out of you when you're dead. I'll only eat your INSIDES. I'll leave your skin pretty and clear and I'll fill you up with teddy bear fluff."

Cara races around a corner, and Lizzie has to stick out a combat boot and kick off one of the shelves to keep from dumping the motorcycle. Her screams take on an even more hysterical pitch; spit flying from her ruby-painted lips.

"MOMMY IS GETTING UPSET; MOMMY WANTS HER VEAL, STOP RUNNING YOU LITTLE BITCH!"

The chopper's engine roars even louder, becoming a final death rattle as the front wheel is mere feet away from running Cara down. Two things happen at once to stop the Vincent Black Shadow from smashing into the child. Mallory dives from behind a filing cabinet and grasps Cara in her arms, knocking the little girl out of harm's way, both of them rolling across the carpet on the far side of the aisle. The second after Mallory's dive Asher bursts back into the fray and buries the head of his silver hatchet into Lizzie's shoulder, causing the madwoman to lose control of the motorcycle, the bike skidding across the carpet before stalling. Lizzie tumbles from the seat and smashes up against a concrete wall, and Luther is right there to push with all of his weight against one of the metal bookshelves, knocking it down in an avalanche of hardbacks, the shelf falling forward and pinning Lizzie up against the wall from the chest up.

Lizzie flails against the shelf, trying to push it off of her to escape her pinned position, and she's even managing to lift it a few inches before Asher darts forward and stabs forward with a silver kitchen knife, impaling Lizzie's hand up against the wall. The madwoman shrieks, and Asher answers this with another assault, this time a gleaming meat fork into her only free hand, stabbing downward and piercing it through her palm and into the side of the bookshelf. Tendrils of smoke rise up from Lizzie's wounds, her crucified hands and the hatchet still wedged deeply in the meat of her shoulder.

She glares at Asher, froth oozing from the sides of her mouth like a rabid animal backed into a corner. She snaps at him with her elongated teeth, but he easily steps out of the range, the madwoman rendered helpless by the silver instruments that bind her.

Her rage becomes a resigned sigh, breathless and pained, her irises changing back and forth from turquoise to yellow, as though she can't control it when in this state of extreme distress. Asher thinks to himself that she resembles some large, deadly insect that has found itself stuck to a strand of sticky fly paper.

"No...fair. You fucking meat forked me, Mister."

Lizzie wiggles the hand with the silver meat fork sticking out of it, the smoke still rising, her flesh looking horribly swollen and red around the wound. The madwoman's face becomes childishly sullen, both Mallory and Cara rising to their feet to stare at her pinned up against the wall.

"I was only gonna eat a tiny bit of you, little girl. Only a few fingers and toes. I'm a nice lady...I swear...I'm a nice...," Lizzie trails off, the shock of the silver affecting her system seeming to drive her into a state of unconsciousness. Her head lolls as she passes out, her black ringlets bobbing.

Asher turns back to Mallory, a deep exhale exiting his mouth. He was deathly afraid they wouldn't be quick enough. He almost thought Cara was lost to them. It was so damn close.

"Cover her eyes," says Asher. Mallory heeds his words, turning Cara away so that she won't see what comes next. Asher reaches deep within his vest and pulls out another blade, this one a serrated silver hunting knife, likely something a collector had commissioned special from the silversmith. He lifts the blade into the air, aiming to drive it as deeply as he can into the madwoman's temple...but Luther's hand lands on his shoulder to stop him.

"Leave her, Asher. She's not going anywhere and there's no time. The albino will come next. We want to be far away from here before that happens."

Asher considers the old man's words, pausing for a moment with the blade raised in midair. Finally he relents, returning the knife to his vest and motioning towards the shattered remnants of the library's front doors.

"You're right. Let's get the hell out of here."

The survivors rush towards the exit, the stink of burnt rubber and hot lycanthrope blood curling into their nostrils as they go.

31

Asher

We're running down barren streets, all of us still processing the events of the last few minutes. None of us have been allowed to properly grieve for the ones we've lost. It's go, go, go...or risk being added to the giant corpse pile in Endre's den.

Luther struggles to keep up, the old man breathing hard, his face florid from the act of fleeing the library. I've taken Cara up into my own arms, holding the little girl with Mallory galloping at my side. Mallory's movements are swift, her body toned and graceful, that blonde hair whipping out behind her as she matches my pace. Tears are streaming down her cheeks. I'm not even sure if she's aware of the fact that she's crying. I imagine she's thinking about Grady and what we allowed the boy to do. That thought haunts me too, a hard knot in my throat that just doesn't go away.

Mallory turns to me, realizing suddenly that we're running towards North Mountain instead of the only road leading out of town.

"Where are we going, Asher? There's nothing up there but wilderness."

"I know those woods, Mallory. We might have a chance up there. We can find a place to hide Cara and—"

I'm never allowed to finish my sentence. A loud whistling sound emerges from one of the crooked side streets we just passed. It sounds like someone blowing on a bone-flute, some hellish note that hangs in the air and taunts, a melody you desperately want to clamp your eardrums against. The albino is close. I can feel his closeness like the approaching of some ancient, abominable force moving with the wind.

I divert our route, moving to a brownstone and whipping up the old wooden doors leading to the house's basement. I quickly hand Cara off to Mallory, motioning for my companions to head down into that cobweb-decorated darkness.

"You have to hide. He hasn't seen us yet. Please don't argue. Just go..."

Mallory's eyes plead with me, her bottom lip quivering. Luther pulls at her, trying to guide her into the basement, the old man seeming to realize the gravity of the situation.

"Where will you go? What will you...do?"

She reaches for me, her hand trembling, and I grasp it firmly in my own. She squeezes it with everything she has. She squeezes it as though she wants to remember what the texture of my skin feels like in case she never gets the chance to feel it again. I struggle to think of a response. It comes out weak, almost lost, but in real life the heroes can't always speak with infallible confidence. And who am I kidding, anyways? I'm a hermit, not a hero...

"I'll distract him. I'll lead him away. I'll try...to end this."

I reach out just once, my hands running along Mallory's cascade of soft, lush hair. My fingers trace that hair, my thumb brushing just slightly against the bottom of her earlobe. She reaches up and holds my hand there, pressing it hard against her cheek, almost like she wishes the handprint would become a tattoo that she'd have forever.

Words betray us now. There is nothing left to say to make this any easier. The moment passes and we disentangle from our desperate, seeking embrace...and Luther and Cara vanish down those rickety steps. Mallory vanishes too; her marigold-colored hair the last shining sight I see before that too is robed in the blackness.

I quietly shut the old wooden doors and place a nearby hunk of cinderblock on top of them. A poor locking mechanism, but it's the best I can put together now. I walk back through a few little side yards until I reach the road. Strangely enough, I'm at the same spot in the road where I originally came down the mountain to return a few library books. My ATV is still sitting there, undisturbed.

The only new thing is the tall figure that stands several yards down the road from me, waiting, whistling, hands shoved down casually into the pockets of his jeans.

32

Crossroads

He stands there in the road like a solitary sentinel, a constant traveler in shredded jeans, his upper torso wearing only the grooves of his own untold scars. There's a considerable distance between both Endre and Asher, the men separated by several yards. Endre makes no move to close that distance yet.

The wind picks up, blowing tangled white hair against the albino's stony features, only a single flash of scarlet eye staring towards the hermit from the hills.

The albino's voice breaks the silence, his hands still casually shoved into his pockets, that ominous whistle dying in the corridors of his throat.

"What's your name, pilgrim?"

Asher considers the question. What's the point of lying now? They're just two men standing on opposite sides of the road, no more hiding, no more plots. Asher realizes his own mistake the moment it enters his mind. He should not think of this figure as a man—it is so much older, so much worse....than just a man.

"Asher."

The albino nods, clicking his tongue against his teeth for a moment. He tilts his head upwards; seeming to relish in what little light the crescent moon offers him before the dark clouds overtake it. The pale illumination paints his equally pale face, features carved skull-like by wind and washed in the waters of the rivers of the world.

"Where's my Lizzie?"

Asher stands his ground across the road, his fists slowly clenching and unclenching at his sides.

"She's not in a position to help you now."

Endre nods, as though he expected as much, and a hollow laugh drifts across the road towards Asher's ears.

"It tickles me that you would presume I need help, Asher."

He pauses, digging an enormous scuffed and ragged boot against the asphalt.

"I've been doing this for a long time. These little genocides, town after town, village after village...and once you've lived as long as I have; you start to just lose count. I was dining on the flesh of humanity when your great-great-grandfather was still just a babe suckling on a titty. Understand the weight of that, Asher. I'm a rambling man, and just when I thought I'd seen it all...Old Hollow happens."

Endre sweeps his white hands from side to side, his skin the color of fissured white parchment.

"Feast after timeless Feast, the results are always the same. I bring my pack into some little shit-stain of a hamlet that's barely on the map. We wait for Mother Moon to give us her harvest blessing, and then we kill and eat every last poor son of a bitch until the population equals zero. We glut ourselves on the cattle of your kind...and then we leave. That's how it's always been."

Endre can't help but grin, shaking his head slightly. The wind plays at his hair, making it like living, twisting tendrils of spider silk flying about his face.

"You and your people....kinda fucked up our familiar routine, don't you see? You decimate my pack. You actually managed to *kill* lycanthropes, beasts so far above you on the food chain that it's comparable to a mouse murdering a lion. But not only that—there's more! You turn one of my own against me. You scheme and plot to assassinate me using one of my own little fuckin' soldier boys. Isn't that rich? Doesn't that just beat all?"

Endre plants his hands on his panther-like hips, staring at Asher incredulously. The albino finally lifts up his palm, signifying that there's a little more he has to get off his barrel of a chest.

"That is impressive, Asher. The very fact that you stand before me now unslaughtered is impressive. Every few hundred years or so I come across one of the cattle that is totally unlike all the others. It's like a prey animal born on the wrong side, a true injustice—because it's so damn obvious this particular animal was meant to be born a predator."

Endre points a pale finger towards Asher, a digit the color of pitted bone. Asher stares back, slate-gray eyes unreadable beneath the clouds that hide the sliver of moon.

"You're not like the rest, are you? I know you're not. I can smell your scent on the wind, Asher, and the scent tells the story of who you are. There's earthy soil beneath your fingernails. There's pure creek water sloshing in your belly. There's woodstove smoke in your hair. Your skin is perfumed in the aromas of the forest, the trees, the ferns, and all those untamed places where man rarely treads. There is no stink of useless technology on you. You don't reek of smartphones, laptops, vain little toys of metal and plastic...all those things that the livestock favor."

Asher looks down at his own hands for a moment. He can't help but notice the dirt grimed beneath his fingernails. He can't help but smell the faintest bit of woodstove smoke from his cabin in his hair and his beard. The scariest part about all of this is that the words of this monster are truthful...

"You're a stranger among them, Asher. I think in the secret corridors of your heart...you know that, don't you? It's not your fault. You were just born on the wrong side. It's fixable."

Endre takes a step or two closer, approaching Asher like an old friend would approach another across the road. Asher's hand creeps towards one of the ATV's handlebars, his body tensed and cautious.

"I see the wildness in you, son. It's just locked inside, and it requires the proper key. I could kill you here on this night road. I could paint the asphalt with your entrails and drink down the creek water that's still splashing in your stomach. I don't want to do that, Asher. There is no need for me to do that..."

Endre sighs, an eldritch sound. He sounds so genuine, actually a bit tired and weary. Those scarlet eyes lock onto Asher, imploring him to look deeper. Asher can almost see endless red wildernesses swirling in those irises...

"Let me give you the bite. I can't offer you immortality, that belongs to the classy corpses with their cute little fangs, but I can offer you lifetimes stacked atop lifetimes. I can give you power that is bottomless. I can connect you with Mother Moon and guide you into becoming the predator that you were always *meant* to be. Forsake the livestock, Asher. Make a meal of the pitiful, delicate cattle...it'll be a mercy to them."

Asher breathes deeply through his nose, his throat constricting as he swallows. These temping words are like fishhooks trying to catch in the inner lining of his cheeks. The thing that disgusts him the most is that a part of him—some primitive, animal part of him—actually LONGS for this promise of freedom in the forests, society left behind, the wild places his new kingdom to be explored and conquered.

The albino seems to notice the effect he's having, a toothy grin spreading across those porcelain cheeks.

"There's a lone wolf inside of you already, Asher. I can practically see the snout pressing against the flesh where your heart beats. He's hungry for the flesh of those carrion critters that are beneath him. Let him come out and play..."

Endre walks closer, those teeth elongating, that lantern-glow starting to eclipse the pink hues of his albinistic eyes.

"Let him eat. Let him feed. Let him *feast*..."

Asher's voice finally stops the great white wolf from progressing closer. It's a single word, decisive, final, dripping with conviction.

"No."

Asher takes in the look of surprise on Endre's face, using that momentary distraction to speak once more.

"You can paint it however you like, but what you are is an abomination. You're a slavering, thoughtless killer...and I would die before seeing myself become the monster that you are."

Endre's lips are peeling back from his teeth, little bristles of white hair starting to sprout out from the flesh of his back. The claws are coming from his fingers, bony knives seeking to disembowel.

"You've torn through this town like a contagious virus, but I'll do everything within my lowly "cattle" power to save what is left of Old Hollow. I'll stand up for this town even though it's not my home, Endre. You're a territorial beast, aren't you? You understand a thing or two about protecting your territory..."

Asher has already climbed atop the ATV, his hand motioning towards that great, black dome in the distance, the forested summit of North Mountain.

"That's my home up there. That's my territory. That...is where we finish this."

Asher fires up the ATV and spins around on the handlebars, the off-road vehicle tearing up the road that steadily leads up the length of the mountain. Endre bays out a glass-shattering howl, shedding his human form completely, the wolf within bursting out in an eruption of snout, claws, teeth and snow-white fur. He clambers down on all fours, racing after the ATV, heavy, hardened paws smashing down against the road and leaving cracks in the asphalt. Saliva splatters from his blackened lips as he shakes his shaggy head from side to side, the hunt heating up his blood and spurring him on.

Asher rides as hard and as fast as he can, the trees flying by on either side of him on the broken old road that leads up the mountain.

The wolf is never far behind...

***

The road climbs steadily upward, the terrain turning from cracked asphalt to hard packed dirt with weeds encroaching on either side. Asher pushes the ATV with absolutely everything he has, leaning forward and trying to literally outrun the devil at his back. The rugged machine blazes forward, soil and pebbles flying from beneath the wheels, and whenever Asher hazards to gaze over his shoulder he sees the monster is always close behind.

The beast lets its tongue loll, saliva splattering as it smashes up the trail in hot pursuit, those insanely strong shoulders pumping as paws pound across dirt and half-submerged stones. Asher's heart beats even faster as he sees a felled tree in the path, and he's barely able to whip the handlebars to the side and guide the ATV around the slim space that lies across from the tree's spindly, uncovered roots.

The beast that is Endre is less graceful when dealing with the obstacle. The great white wolf simply darts his thick neck beneath the trunk and power lifts it like it's nothing but a sapling, the tree smashing down behind him and rolling back down the mountain trail.

The chase has brought Asher to his cabin, but he has no plans of stopping there. His destination lies deeper in the wilderness, a place near Opequen Creek that is virtually forgotten by everyone except for himself and the wildlife that frequents the ground below. Asher breaks from the main trail, the ATV bouncing across a ravine before the wheels meet the earth again, the off-road vehicle maneuvering between elms and pines that seem almost to touch the sky.

Asher can hear the sound of the creek flowing in the distance. He sees that beacon in the shadows, a great edifice of old, rotten wood that stands out against the dark horizon. It was a watchtower once but the local park rangers and game wardens abandoned it and simply never bothered with it again, so it's fallen into terrible disrepair. There's a massive grove beneath it, a clearing bordered on all sides by ancient oaks that have stood as sentinels next to the watchtower for decade after decade.

Asher can't really decide why he came to this place. His primary motivation was to lure Endre as far from Old Hollow as possible, and this mountain clearing is about as isolated as it gets, far above town, far from the people that still desperately cling to life down there in the valley below.

In his wolfen form, Endre never seems to tire. Asher brings the ATV to a sudden stop in the clearing, hopping from the seat of the ATV to locate his pursuer. He doesn't have to wait long. Endre bursts from between the trunks of two great oaks, leaving ragged claw marks across the bark while offering Asher his largest lupine grin, seeming simply to tease him.

Asher buries a hand into the pocket of his vest and pulls out a thick silver letter opener, taking a moment to aim with precision and toss the blade in the direction of the approaching lycanthrope. Asher has always been an ace when it comes to knife throwing; he'd even consider it one of his finest mountain talents...something he's practiced for years in these lonely woodlands. He's a bull's eye shot almost every single time.

Not this time. Endre reaches up a paw and swats the letter opener out of the sky like it's a bothersome fly that dared to venture near his face. The blade clatters off somewhere in the underbrush, lost and useless. The mammoth of a werewolf actually speaks to Asher in his wolfen form, the syllables coming out in a mixture of snarls and ragged growls, words emerging from vocal cords twisted and rearranged by the transformation.

"Gotta admire your hubris, son. It is the bane of your species. I'm descended from the line of Fenrir—something you know nothing of—and you'd threaten me with a sharp little envelope-opener?"

The Alpha throws back his shaggy head, his laughter a cacophony of hoots and howls from his throat, the wildlife in the forest fleeing from that sound. Birds flee their nests; raccoons scurry off into the thistles, and deer lope off in terror at the noise of this new predator that has entered into their once peaceful territory.

"You're amusing, cattle-carcass. I'll eat your hands last as a show of respect for that throw. Dexterity makes for excellent dinner..."

Asher knows in the depths of his soul that this is hopeless. If he fights this beast, he will lose...but something within him compels him to at least try. It is better to die fighting than to die cowering. This monster has taken much from Old Hollow, blood, lives, serenity turned to cinders and ruination. But there is one thing Asher will not let this beast feed on. Asher will not give Endre the satisfaction of eating up even a single iota of his fear...

The man rushes the great white wolf, Asher's muscles tensing to grapple...but Endre simply catches him and throws him across the clearing like a lawn dart, Asher's body flying at least ten feet before crushing up against the hard surface of one of the massive oak trees. The bark bites deeply into his side, and as soon as he hits the ground he realizes that several of his ribs are cracked, a terrible, pulsing pain flowing through his chest. Asher's face is pressed deeply into spongy moss, his breath coming out in short, clipped bursts.

He starts to crawl towards a granite boulder, his arms reaching up to pull against the surface of the rock, every breath a struggle now as the pain blooms into wretched roses within his rib cage. Asher finally finds his feet, leaning heavily against the granite while clutching to his sides, and Endre saunters over, his looming, gargantuan form like a pure white polar bear venturing forward to make a meal of an unfortunate seal.

The albino swipes out with a single paw aimed at Asher's throat, but the intended victim is able to just duck out of the way and shamble to the side. Endre's sharpened bone claws literally shred through the granite, pieces of the rock flying around like shrapnel. Meanwhile Asher has stumbled his way over to the wooden ladder leading up to the rickety old watchtower, and he starts to climb as fast as he can, ascending with his teeth gritted against the anguish in his chest. Rung after laborious rung, he finally manages to crawl out across the surface of the tower's top, using the weakening railing to pull himself back up to his feet. The watchtower itself is gutted, most of the outer walls broken and crumbling, leaving just a sort of platform at the top that is currently being rocked ever so slightly by the night wind.

The tallest of the oak trees in the grove is rooted right next to the tower; many sturdy branches reaching over to seemingly caress the old failing edifice. Nature reclaiming man's creation, the fate of all man-made things in the end. Asher sways in the night wind, his body racked with pain. Endre is already coming up to meet him, the great white wolf bounding up the ladder in incredible leaps that shake the entire foundation even more.

Asher thinks perhaps he can manage to grab hold of the beast—a final hug—and pitch both of them off the railing to the ground below. Surely the fall won't kill Endre, but it might wound him, even lame him for a time. As long as it gives Mallory, Luther, and Cara a chance to escape, his own death will be worth it. All further planning withers from his mind now.

The beast has climbed atop the watchtower. The beast is with him. A tongue slips out, impossibly long, licking at a maw that craves the taste of worthy cattle-flesh. The flesh of a rebellious warrior is always the sweetest kind...and Endre's belly rumbles with the promised supper that stands before him.

A serrated sentence falls from behind row after row of equally serrated teeth.

"And so the hunt ends."

"So it does," Asher replies, his bearded visage lowering. Does he even have the strength to pull this unfathomably strong creature over the railing with him? It feels like his chest is full of broken shards of stone...

Endre approaches, taking his time, his hind legs carrying him across the platform with bone claws carving little rivets in the wood beneath his feet.

"You've been good sport, Asher. So many long, monotonous centuries of existence. So many hunts. I'm rarely met with opposition of your caliber. You love this mountain, don't you?"

Asher takes a moment to look around him—a final moment—and he nods his agreement to the question. He can just see the few remaining lights of Old Hollow in the valley far below the forested slopes. North Mountain has nurtured him. It has given him solace apart from society—a sanctuary all his own.

"I do...with my whole heart."

Endre nods, one pallid paw reaching forward to latch itself around Asher's throat. The lycanthrope doesn't apply any real pressure; he doesn't immediately squeeze the throat to pulp even though he could. He seems to enjoy prolonging this. Endre is accustomed to having lesser beings rendered impotent and defeated in the palms of his ancient hands.

"It is beautiful country, untamed, still wild. It won't last, though. I've lived long enough to know. Such places never last."

Endre starts to apply pressure now, those bone-colored digits pressing against Asher's windpipe, constricting his airflow bit by bit until he struggles for each little inhalation of the night wind.

"After I have devoured and digested you, I will shit out a little pile of your bones in front of that cabin we passed on the way up here. Consider it a consolation. I honor you by letting a few remnants of your body mix with the soil of your mountain."

Asher turns his face away from the beast's mockery, focusing on the twisting branches of the oak tree that embrace the forsaken watchtower, two old lovers made of wood holding desperately to one another. For a brief moment, he thinks he sees eyes flashing through the leaves. Familiar eyes. Golden eyes...

He thinks for a moment that it's simply a hallucination brought on by deprived oxygen, but no, *she* is there. The noise from the watchtower has woken her from her languid slumber, and she moves so quietly across the wide limb of the oak, padding forward like a hunched, lethal ghost hidden in the leaves. Endre does not notice her approach...or even her scent. He's too busy pressing his flaring snout along the length of my perspiring cheek, drinking in the aroma of my helplessness.

She was frail and small when I saw her that morning seemingly a lifetime ago. Just a starving cub when I threw her those fish and watched her gobble them up in seconds. She is large and muscular now, an apex predator that has chosen her own slice of territory atop North Mountain. We are intruding on that territory.

Endre never sees her coming. The mountain lion pounces from behind the leaves like a murderous missile, falling atop the lycanthrope with hooked claws and canine teeth like miniature daggers. She shrieks as she thrashes him, tearing and ripping at his face, one of her hooked claws swiping downward so violently that she cleanly clips off half of the lycanthrope's ear. She goes for the throat bite next, the killing blow...but Endre's power is simply too much, and he snatches her body from him and throws her back into the branches from whence she came, her body tumbling down the trunk of the oak and scratching furrows into it as she manages to land upright across the ground.

Endre is bleeding profusely from his mangled features, wiping at the blood with his paws, and Asher sees that fate has provided him with the most optimum opening that he will ever get. With the great white wolf distracted, Asher reaches into the pockets of his vest and retrieves the last object he salvaged from the house of the silversmith. It's a common butcher knife, the blade eight inches of gleaming, exquisite silver. Asher rushes towards the enormous werewolf with everything that he has, thrusting the blade in a sweeping arch, the knife plunging through Endre's snow-furred chest right above the heart.

The effect is immediate. Endre's expression contorts, shock showing through the ragged wounds inflicted by the mountain lion. His lantern eyes are flickering, losing strength—starting to return to the pink-hues of his albinistic human form. In that critical moment, after lifetime after lifetime, Endre seems to realize that he has been undone. The lycanthrope performs a final act...reaching out with one of his ragged bone claws in the direction of Asher's right eye, allowing just the tip of that claw to graze Asher's cornea, leaving the slightest little scratch there. A single teardrop of blood oozes from Asher's eye, but he blinks it away painlessly. He barely even notices the scratched cornea or the stretching, semi-satisfied smile that passes across Endre's lupine face. Asher simply sinks the butcher knife in a little deeper, an acrid smoke billowing out from the wound, and with one flick of the wrist, Asher twists the blade in the albino's heart.

Endre's lupine form drifts away, his features returning to that of his guise of humanity...all pale, scarred skin, long white hair, and scarlet-colored eyes. He stumbles backwards, taking a moment to look down at the hilt of the blade that has been embedded in his chest. He's still puzzling over this fatal wound—a wound inflicted by one of the cattle—when his body connects with the rotten railing behind him and it gives away, his giant form plummeting downward at breakneck speed, flipping and somersaulting through the air.

His carcass lands with a huge splash in the waters of Opequen Creek, all the glimmering, feral light dying in the crimson orbs of his eyes. The Alpha dethroned. The Father of the Feast...felled and finished.

The current of the Opequen carries his corpse away...

***

Asher leans heavily against the railing, barely believing that he remains alive and Endre is now just a dead husk floating down the creek. He suffers no visual impairment from the tip of Endre's claw dragging lightly against his cornea. His ribs even feel better, almost like sudden warmth is traveling through his chest, soothing the damage that was done there.

He gazes down into the clearing and catches sight of the mountain lion for just a moment, her body partially obscured by a smattering of ferns. She looks to be unhurt, her graceful form managing to navigate her safely down the tree trunk even after Endre threw her. They lock eyes from a distance. Man staring into the heart of Nature herself. Even though he knows his human tongue cannot communicate with something so beautiful, so wild, and so perfectly primal...he still whispers down to her regardless.

"Thank you."

She gives him the gift of her golden gaze for a few seconds longer, and then she slinks off into the forest, her lithe body vanishing behind the towering oaks. Soon she is gone entirely.

The past repeats itself, and Asher turns his face up to the starlit sky and closes his eyes, silently thanking the universe for being kind.

33

Lizzie

My hands hurt, and my shoulder stings like it was bitten by a thousand mean old horseflies. I had to wiggle like a worm to get the silver pieces out of me, and it took even longer to push that bookshelf up and squeeze myself out from underneath. I licked up the blood from my wounds like a kitty cat does, and that helped a little. I can't purr now. No purring for lost, deserted Lizzie.

I push my motorcycle along the road leading out of this rotten place, this stinky town that ruined our fun and ended our Feast. My hands are bandaged up tight with rags, and the skin is slowly but surely stitching itself back together underneath. It tickles. It feels like butterfly wings flapping in the meat of myself. If Mother Moon gave me butterfly wings, I'd use them to fly away too. I guess I'll just have to ride instead.

My pale prince is dead now. We were connected—whirling spirits of nature, the heartbeat of my mate always throbbing in my own temple. I felt it when he died. Our blood connection severed, Endre's centuries of life dripping away like water from a broken faucet. These fucking cattle bastards, these manure-stained livestock...they took everything from me. My pack. My lover. My fun. I want to tear the nasty cock off the one who killed my Endre and beat him to death with his own phallus.

But I'm hurt now, and I'm alone. I was alone in the asylum too another lifetime ago. They always hurt me there. They said I was full of mania and melancholia and when I got upset, they'd stick me in the rusty cage with the iron bars and I'd rattle those bars all night long. Sometimes they'd wrap me up in the soiled straightjacket and dip me back into a tub filled with ice water, trying to freeze the frenzy out of me. Every night I slept curled up in a ball, just counting my toes and listening to the mutters and the squeals of the others that lived at the asylum.

They said I was a lost cause, a gibbering loon, and they were gonna put the spike through my brain and be done with it. I would have been lobotomized if not for my pale prince. He saved me, just a shivering damsel in distress, whisking me away from the doctors with their monocles and their moustaches and their cold, probing fingers.

Endre gave me the gift of a new life. He worked his fascinating sorcery in the deep, dark woods and he put a wolf inside of me. He put a snarling, furious thing inside of me that I can let out whenever Mother Moon becomes full, and I felt so empowered, a brand new woman. No more padded rooms with messages smeared in shit on the walls. No more listening to slobbering idiots being pushed around in creaky old wheelchairs.

I was free, deliciously free. We'd fuck under the stars on a bed of pine needles, and he'd nibble my neck and give me rough kisses and leave such handprints etched into my flesh. I'll miss his rough, ragged kisses. I'll miss being fucked from behind with my face pressed against the moss, my tongue slipping out to lick at the snails that crawled slowly by. I'll miss my pale prince so very much...

All the other towns were just playpens. The people there were just breakfast, lunch, and dinner for our pack. This damned Old Hollow is cursed. The cattle shouldn't ever kill our kind. We are superior. We are the nomadic wolves of the world.

I hope Endre made it to the Great Forest that lies beyond. I hope he's running beneath the pines that touch the sky, and I only wish I had some wolfsbane petals to place overtop his eyes. His body is long gone now, though...and I can never keep the wolfsbane petals he gives me. I always nibble and snack on them. Silly Lizzie. SILLY FUCKING LIZZIE!

I start up the motorcycle, the engine loud and soothing in my ears. I hop up onto the seat and guide the bike around the eighteen wheeler that blocks the road. I let the chopper tear down the highway, the wind blowing through my hair.

I want to get far away from this town. I want to heal and lick my wounds for a long time. I hate this Old Hollow. I want to pour salt on the people left there like slugs and I want to kick and stomp them until their faces turn to soupy mush.

I hate this Old Hollow so much.

And when the time is right, I will come back...and show these cattle just how deep and wide the cauldron of my hatred is.

34

Asher

Night fades during my trip back down the mountain, the sunlight sending fresh rays slanting through the treetops. That sunlight feels good on my face, warming my soul, seeming to bathe away the horrors of the last few days.

The ATV is rumbling down the trail, jolting my body up and down as I cling to the handlebars. This should be sending shockwaves of pain through my ribs. It doesn't. The pain in my chest is distant, replaced by a sensation like bones knitting inside of me. It's a warm feeling, just as warm as the sunlight playing across my skin. The excruciation I felt during the fight with Endre is fading—being replaced by a sense of growing strength, the scents of North Mountain taking on entirely new spectrums.

I know what that means. I now understand why Endre reached out so desperately to graze the tip of that claw across my eye before his fall, such a subtle, guileful movement. A final "fuck you" from the treacherous old monster...a gift I never asked for.

I sigh, my head hanging low. The fate of Old Hollow is secure now, but my own fate remains obscure. The sound of that sigh seems to reverberate in my own eardrums, a powerful vibration as my hearing is starting to become hypersensitive.

The wolves didn't win in this lonely mountain town...

But they succeeded in making me one of them.

***

I pull the ATV up to the brownstone, taking time to hop off the seat and toss the cinderblock away from the outer basement doors. I call down to them, and I'm met with a little toddler missile that plants sloppy kisses all over my cheeks and forehead. I lift Cara and spin her around for a moment, Mallory and Luther both emerging together from the darkness. Mallory struggles to hold back tears, her hand reaching up to brush against her lips. Luther reaches out a gnarled hand to grip my shoulder, the librarian surprisingly strong despite his age.

There's this unexplainable feeling in the air, a sense that a dark cloud has finally parted over Old Hollow and happiness is allowed to grow here again. Somehow Mallory and Luther seem to know it in their hearts without me even having to tell them. Even little Cara feels it, the child perhaps the most intuitive of us all.

"Remember you told me bout' the knights, Asher?"

I can't help but smile as she plays with my collar, my body crouched down before the little girl with a dirty face and spider webs in her hair.

"I remember."

"Did they win? Did we...win?"

I pull Cara deeper into my arms, my hands brushing the cobwebs out of her hair. She doesn't shiver in fear beneath cold moonlight anymore. Now she blooms in the sun.

"The knights won, Cara. The monsters are gone."

I pick the little girl up, setting her atop an oversized rocking chair on the porch of the brownstone. She sits there like a little queen that has just inherited a kingdom of roses, swaying her self back and forth in the rocking chair.

Mallory comes forth next, her hand fluttering out to touch my arm, her eyes imploring. I suppose my face tells most of the story, but my introverted tongue struggles to tell her the rest.

"It's over now, Mallory. I killed Endre...with the help of an old friend. He's gone. His Feast is finished here now."

Mallory's sweet face seems to contort, half-choked sobs emerging from her throat. The freckles on her face look like beautiful constellations to me, and I wish I could explore each and every one of them with my fingertips. Luther's voice finds me next.

"The lunatic managed to free herself. We heard her start up that motorcycle of hers even from the dankness of this basement. I listened to the sound of the engine...and it drifted out of Old Hollow. I believe she left town."

I nod, surmising as much. Perhaps it was a mistake not to finish the madwoman, but it's too late to worry about that now.

"I don't think we'll need to concern ourselves with her anytime soon. Her pack is dead and her alpha is lost to her...she won't dare return when she's wounded and outnumbered. Endre's leadership was the only thing that allowed her to function, and without that direction, her lack of sanity will likely undo her sooner rather than later."

Our conversation is put on halt by something extremely surreal happening from various points along the road. People are emerging from hidey-holes, some of them drifting out from beneath crawlspaces, a few wandering out of the woods bordering the town, there's even a stocky father that pushes up a manhole cover and lifts his two sons up before climbing out himself. All of these lost souls, the survivors of Old Hollow—people that have been hiding and hoping ever since this nightmare began. They look confused, hungry, and cored out by the dark visitors that tore through their town. More and more keep appearing, a young woman climbing down from a tall pine near the post office, a couple stumbling out from the back of an SUV with the back window painted in mud camouflage.

I guess they feel it just like we feel it. The nightmare has passed, as nightmares often do, and now it's finally time to awaken. They whisper to one another in the sunlight, separated families finding each other again and clinging to one another in the middle of the road.

All of us watch this in awe for a few moments, and then something dawns on me. I return to my ATV and reach deeply into the satchel along the back, taking up a stack of books and placing them firmly in the hands of the librarian that walked through Hell with me. Luther can only gape, his grin spreading across his wrinkled face like a brushstroke across a weathered canvas.

"I hope you won't charge me a late fee under the circumstances, old friend."

Luther laughs heartily, the sound welcome and lasting. He hugs the books to his chest, even bringing them up to his nose to take in the scent of them. I can smell them too. The aroma comes to me like incense through my nostrils, old paper, well loved pages, and binding made to last. I've always loved the smell of books...but the scent has never been stronger than it is for me in this moment among my friends, just one little ragged group of survivors among many in the heart of Old Hollow.

"Since you've saved my withered ass, consider it waived, young Asher. We bibliophiles live to read another day..."

Mallory waits in the road, the sunlight seeming to catch in that marigold hair, turning it to bright, blazing glory. I go to her, my heart heavy, the biggest part of the story about what happened on North Mountain still left unsaid. I wish I didn't have to say it. I want nothing more than to fall into her freckled arms and stay there forever, holding her warmth, pressing my face against her hair. My thoughts drift towards dreams of growing old together in Old Hollow, watching that golden hair turn gray, our souls only binding together more firmly with the passage of time.

I can't grow old now. That luxury was robbed from me, and despite his demise, Endre has piled lifetime after lifetime onto my soul—a soul that has already felt comfortably old since the moment of my birth.

Mallory reaches her thumbs into the bands of my jeans and pulls me in closer, our faces inches apart. She knows something is troubling me. She sees the storm clouds in my eyes and she's desperately trying to understand why they're there at all.

"What's the matter, Asher? We're free now. We made it through this. *You* guided us through this horror show...and we've come out on the other side."

I swallow deeply, taking a moment to point up to my right eye, specifically the little slit of scratched cornea that has already begun to heal.

"My eye. Look deeper..."

Mallory squints, leaning forward. I can smell her skin pressing against mine, and it carries with it the faintest scent of lilacs. Her expression first contorts with shock, and next comes the sorrow.

"Endre's claw. Just the tiniest scratch, I barely even felt it, but it was enough. It was enough to turn me..."

"No. Not after all we've been through. Just...no..."

Mallory breaks down, falling into my arms, and I catch her, my hand running through her hair as she cries against my chest.

I whisper down to her, letting my lips brush just slightly against her ear.

"I'll have to go away for awhile, Mallory. I can't endanger this town after everything that's happened here. I have to learn to control the beast that lives inside of me now. Grady wasn't like the others. He learned to master the wolf within, and I promise you, I will do the same. Grady said it was all about compromises. You have to find the balance between the man you were and the animal you've become..."

I reach down, tilting Mallory's chin up so that I can meet her eyes. I wipe the tears from her cheeks with my thumbs. I can smell the saltiness of them—the scent of sadness that is swirling in her heart.

"I'll come with you, Asher. Let Cara and I—"

She breaks off, realizing the futility of her statement, and the sobs come again.

"Listen to me, Mallory. This is not goodbye. Once I've learned to control what I am, I will find my way back to you. I'll come back to Old Hollow. But right now, these people—all these lost, scared people—they need a leader. They need someone to help them pick up the pieces and guide them into rebuilding their town. They need a loud, strong voice to show them the way."

Mallory stops crying, her features taking on a hard, determined expression. This is the woman who fought off Raymond and prevented the sick freak from raping her. This is the warrior that killed the first of Endre's pack with a mixture of silver and lion-heart courage.

"That person is you, Mallory. They're going to need you."

She nods, nibbling on her bottom lip just slightly.

"You promise you'll come back to me? We can carve out a place all our own on your mountain—a cabin or a mansion, it's all the same to me. Just as long as you're there."

I can't help but chuckle, a low, quiet sound. I try to hide my own sorrow, but it's still there, a burning in my chest that hurts worse than the cracked ribs ever did.

"I am wealthy in words, but that is all. Cabin, mansion, castle...whatever you want, we'll find a way. I'll be there. *We'll* be there... and every night when the crickets chirp and the frogs sing, we'll look down from our mountain at Old Hollow...and we'll see the little town that so many of us fought and died to save."

I find myself lost in the deep pools of Mallory's eyes, so brightly green, eyes full of soul and stony resolve. She's lived the hardscrabble life of struggle and strife in these West Virginia hills, and that shines through in her gaze. I find it incredibly attractive. I pull her towards me, my hands lingering on her hips while her own arms reach around the back of my neck, coiling and pulling me close, those graceful fingers of hers twirling in my coal-black hair.

The kiss tastes as sweet as honey, her lips like nectar sending shivers of pleasure down my spine. I wish it could last forever—captured in time, those soft lips pressing against my own with the sunlight dancing across our skin. The passion ensnares, my hands finding her cheeks while my thumbs lightly trace the delicate lines of her ears. She is everything that I want, this golden-haired goddess, and it takes great willpower to finally break the kiss and let our lips come apart. Her cheeks are flushed as red as roses, and this only serves to make her seem more magical...standing there in the road, my heart captured by every aspect of her.

I will master this wolf within. I will come back to Old Hollow.

I'll bring balance to the beastly urges, and I will do it for *her*.

Luther has overhead most of this, hanging back and allowing us this intimate moment. The old man comes forward now, thrusting a first edition book into my hands. I look down at the intricate cover, smiling. It's Mary Shelley's "Frankenstein".

"Take it. It was always your favorite..."

"Thank you."

I embrace the old man, taking in his scent—the aroma of a grandfather fond of telling tales before a roaring fireplace. Cara has come down from her rocking chair now, and I crouch down to lightly kiss the child's forehead. I can almost picture her in a full suit of armor riding atop a white steed. She'll always be a little knight to me.

I climb atop the ATV and I start the engine, heading down the only road leading out of Old Hollow. I look back only once.

My own little pack of survivors...standing tall, watching me go.

Epilogue

The Yukon

Several months later...

Asher stands with his eyes closed, his mind in a state of extreme concentration. He feels the dark, earthy soil beneath his bare feet. He hears the night wind blowing through the towering black spruce trees that dominate the landscape all around him, some of the needles drifting down to light like moths across his muscular shoulders. Artic lupines grow in patches all around this particular hill, purple flowering petals reaching Asher's highly sensitive nostrils, intoxicating him, making him sway slightly on his feet.

He begins to hum, a calming mechanism that he's found helps before the change. He hears the Yukon River flowing lazily somewhere to the north, helping him to focus on the soothing serenity of the cool, cleansing water. He thinks Grady must have felt this way in the early days.

This was the paradise where Grady came to terms with what he'd become, and now it's the paradise Asher has sought out to do the same.

The aurora borealis is flashing across a sky that seems endless, painting the night in a kaleidoscope of color, purples, reds, and eerily haunting greens. Asher can feel her rising higher beyond the northern lights, her cratered call singing to his soul. She whispers through the evergreens. She makes the artic lupines dance in the breeze. Mother Moon. Run. Hunt. Be a wild thing in a wild place. These are her messages from above...

Asher feels his bones rearranging inside of him. He feels the coal-black fur sprouting up out of his flesh, slowly, a few strands leading to a lush coat. The claws are pushing forth out of his fingertips, his face contorting, becoming a muzzle full of sharp, porcelain-colored teeth.

The moonbeams break through the clouds, kissing his face...

Asher opens his eyes.

Eyes that glow like internal lanterns, a glow to match the moonbeams. The wolf is here. The wolf is free.

Afterword

I love werewolves. I always have, ever since I was a little boy. The myth of lycanthropy has always enchanted me, this idea of transformation and becoming a wild thing governed only by nature and the rising of the moon. Wolves in general have always captured my interest—pretty obvious since I have a wolf tattoo on my left bicep. I'm intrigued by the concept of the hierarchy within a pack, the concept of lone wolves...just everything about the species. Of all supernatural creatures, werewolves are the ones that speak to me the most as a writer, and I felt it was only a matter of time before I cobbled together my own tale and take on lycanthropes.

My intention with this novel was to showcase how animalistic, savage, and just plain *scary* werewolves can be...these hulking, bestial monsters that can make mincemeat of puny mortals that cross paths with them. I started thinking about a certain albino alpha, and that thought lead to a certain dreadful Feast...

I hope I did the lycanthrope myth justice with this book and provided a bit of a fresh spin on the old folklore of a man transforming into a beast. I can honestly say that I had a great deal of fun writing this story and getting into the headspace of characters like Asher, Endre, Mallory, Grady...and so many others.

In closing, as long as my imagination keeps cooking up the horror, I'll keep serving it to any and all readers who enjoy walks through the dark, tangled forest paths of spooky fiction.

Thanks for joining me on this particular walk, my fellow horror junkies.

ABOUT THE AUTHOR:

When I was still a child and picked up my very first Goosebumps book by R. L. Stine, I knew I'd fallen head over heels in love with all things horror. It's a love affair that has only grown stronger over the years, a borderline obsession with stories that explore the darkest recesses of the human imagination. I guess you could say I'm like Thorny Rose in that way...always stalking down those special stories that have the ability to invoke a creepy-crawly feeling right down in the marrow of my bones.

As I grew older I discovered the work of some of my biggest inspirations like Stephen King, Edgar Allan Poe, H.P. Lovecraft, Clive Barker...and the work of those authors sent me deeper down the path of the macabre. During my teenage years I had the little tradition of reading Stephen King's The Stand each summer to lose myself in the devastation of the superflu and marvel at the sadistic magnetism of Randall Flagg.

I've devoured horror fiction for as long as I can remember and reading the words weaved by the greats of the genre inspired me to begin writing. I wanted the opportunity to tell my own tales with the intent to terrify, to disturb; to capture the morbid curiosity of the reader just as my own was caught so early on in life.

If I've managed to inspire some of those feelings in you, my readers, then I feel that I've accomplished something just a little bit magical. There's still some magic left in this world, and I think it's most powerful when manifested in the form of words scrawled across many blank pages. Granted any magic contained within my work will be of the dark variety...but I wouldn't want it any other way. ;)

Jeremy Megargee lives in Martinsburg, West Virginia. When he's not writing, he enjoys hiking mountain trails, weight training, getting tattooed and being a garden variety introvert in his mid-20s. Oh, and reading too (duh).

Megargee is also the author of DIRT LULLABIES, SWEET TREATS, BURNT SCROLLS, AND WORDS FOR CROWS.

Connect with me online:

Facebook: www.facebook.com/JMHorrorFiction

Instagram: @xbadmoonrising

Thanks for reading!

What did you think of OLD HOLLOW?

Feedback is incredibly important for indie authors. Most indie authors are not affiliated with Big Publishing and we don't have the vast resources or marketing tools to get our names out there compared to many of the advertised best-selling titles. Reviews give my work additional exposure and help new readers to discover my particular brand of horror.

If you enjoyed this book, I would love it if you could head over to the Amazon.com page for Old Hollow and leave an honest review about what you thought of the book. I read every single review I get and I'm very grateful for the support.

Feel free to share this book with friends, word of mouth advertising goes a long way...and it helps the horror spread. ;)

CPSIA information can be obtained
at www.ICGtesting.com
Printed in the USA
LVHW081327240521
688333LV00022B/760

9 781532 748592